Sanitarium Magazine
Issue no. 40

Thank you to all of our contributors, we couldn't have done it without you.

FACULTY MEMBERS

Dr. Sputnik
Dr. Muratori
Dr. Soldan
Dr Algee
Dr. Marceau
Dr. Warra

Contents

Facing Up by David Gianatasio 7

Breeding In The Spheres by Tyler Tristao 13

The Journal of the Median Man – A Face on the Wall by Barry Price 37

The Cottonwood Curse by John Beechem 71

Jesus Fuck: or The Beheading by Jay Helmstutler 81

Exoskeleton by Martin Ian Smith 89

Cemetery Dead Ahead by Leonard J. Dawson 109

Stacy by Myles Paine 117

The Third Bell by Ryan Leach 129

Leper Writer by Roo Bardookie 147

On The Record 151

    A Moment With Jeff Menapace 153

    A Moment With Dan Sunley: Pieces 159

ISSUE FORTY

Dear Reader,

Season's Greetings to all our readers and I hope you have had your fill of food and drink as we head in to the New Year.

The past 12 months have been an interesting ride, with killer interviews and stories that have stuck with me and this has me looking forward to 2016. More interviews, news, reviews and fiction will follow and we hope you join us for the ride.

This month we have 9 stories, a dark verse and two interviews for you to enjoy.

Happy New Year!

Barry Skelhorn

Facing Up by David Gianatasio

Running past faces. A hundredthousandmillion faces. All blasted. Ruined. Wasted. Horrible, unspeakable, tortured faces. Mutilations. Eyes—oozing pus, trailing stalks, twisted and shot through with milky cataracts. Ears—malformed, hideous, discolored: strange plants waving in the wind, lumps of flesh, clumps of clay, pitiful. Noses—abominations. (Most of the faces would look better if the noses, where included, were removed.) Mouths—twisted in bitter sneers, grimaces of pain. Teeth broken and rotting, tongues swollen, dripping—wastelands of eyesearsnosesmouths.

They watch as I run screaming down Main Street.

Strange; their bodies appear normal. Unscathed, even perfect. That woman there in the summer dress, window-shopping at a clothing store—cool angles and slender curves, slim arms and legs lightly muscled. But that face. It's like the surface of the moon, scarred and pitted. Torn apart. Ears and eyes missing— gaping, pus-filled holes. Three noses. Hair green and slimy. Mouth like a vampire, sharp yellow fangs falling an inch past parted lips—she's smiling at me.

I keep running, panting, legs pumping, heart heaving, tripping over my feet as panic pushes me along.

Past the decapitated traffic cop, hat dancing on a geyser splashing up from his neck. Past Gino's Barber Shop, where Gino pokes out his eyes with a scissors. Past Orlando's Foreign Motors, where Orlando washes his face with battery acid, dries his blistered cheeks with sandpaper squares and oily rags.

I'm normal, by the way. All of me. My body—and my face. It's everyone else who's changed. I woke up today just like every morning since the crash: screeching brakes inside my head, Angie's melting face seared across my memory. Angie's face. It wasn't really a face anymore. It was my fault. Drunk, don't you know. Drunk like always.

My ol' pal Jack D. wouldn't let me keep the car between the lines. I hardly got a scratch. Broken leg, that was all. My face was just fine. My part-time actor's face—unblemished, photogenic, marketable. Handsome—if I say so myself, and I've been told often enough by others to believe it's true. Handsome enough to get me work in that convenience store commercial last year, to win me walk-ons in no fewer than three movies of the week.

The cops said I wasn't legally drunk, so there wasn't even a trial or counseling. Just an accident, a horrible mistake.

Angie's face was way past repair. Six surgeries didn't help. No more auditions for Angie, no more photo shoots or casting calls. She was a model. Wouldn't it figure—made her living from her face.

And I was sorry. God, I was sorry. You've got to believe me: I was, I was! I mean... I still am. Sorry. It's true and I don't know why nobody believes me, why her folks and even mine won't believe me. I'm sorry, dammit! How freaking sorry am I supposed to be? Sorry forever? Sure, whatever. I'm sorry... OK? I've tried to stay on the wagon and sure I shouldn't have been driving and I went to AA for Chrissakes and maybe I am drinking again, but so freaking what?! It's my right to be as sorry as I wanna be and who are you to judge?

One day I came home and found her swinging from the ceiling like a lean side of beef. (Sorry, so sorry. But I didn't tie the noose and kick the stool out from under her feet! You think I'm not hurting, too, you stupid bastards! Sure, I'd told her I was leaving... but... Look at what I did to her! Why stay? I'd ruined her. And besides, Jesus Christ, I just couldn't take it, couldn't stand to look for one more minute at that scarred, distorted face!)

That was months ago.

Then I woke up this morning. Started shaving, removing unsightly hairs from my weathered-but-could-pass-for-ten-years-younger face. I switched on the TV and screamed. I haven't stopped screaming since. The anchorwoman was a talking skeleton—no flesh at all, just a yakking jawbone, gleaming white. The weather guy had half a face—bits of his brain kept splashing across his meteorological map. Same on every channel—charred faces, ghastly, beyond belief. Surreal parodies of Julia Roberts, Richard Gere, Cindy Crawford and Michael Jordan smiled from the stack of glossy magazines on the coffee table. It was as if a belligerent Dali had risen from the grave and wrought a terrible vengeance on the glitterati, leaving them disfigured but still recognizable beneath the lurid headlines and 18-point type promising the latest scoop on food, fashion and sex.

That's when I ran outside, still in my underwear with bits of lather on my all-too-perfect face. I hit the streets like a lost soul searching for a way out of hell. I don't know where I'm going. I have no idea what to do. But I've got to keep moving. That's the only thing I know for sure ... Because they're coming out of doors and staring from windows. They're not chasing me like they would in some B movie or a childhood nightmare. They're staring (the ones who have eyes), pointing at me. Passing judgment.

"Handsome," they hiss and moan, coming closer, fingers straining to grab.

Handsome means guilty.

The End.

CASE #82712

FACING UP

BY DAVID GIANATASIO

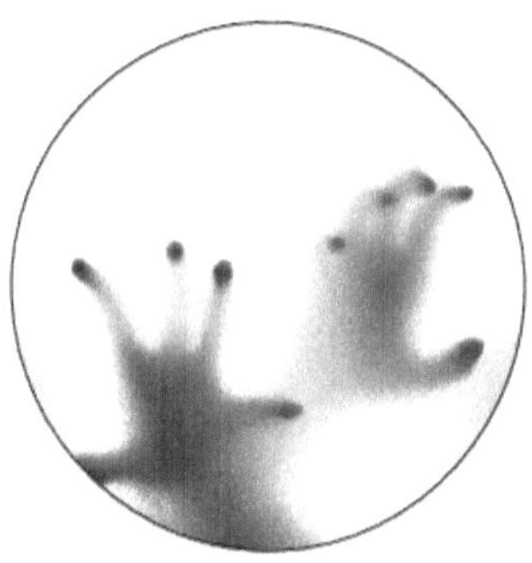

David Gianatasio's fiction, articles and essays often appear in print and online, and he has published two collections of short stories.

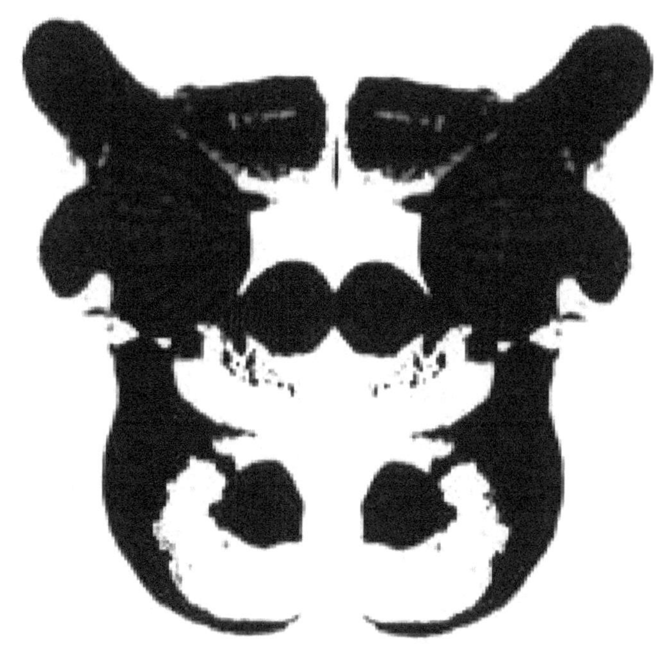

Breeding In The Spheres by Tyler Tristao

"A day will come when two men, not unlike ourselves, will be waiting for the shroud of dusk to fall so that our bodies can be snatched and taken to the good doctor," Veece said. He was leaning against the alley wall, staring at the cobbled ground.

"Do you got to get into this every damn night before we go out with our shovels?" Monte asked. "Seems to me like you should have been a scribe, Veece. You have the darkened mind for philosophy, ye do."

"You're in denial if you stand over a freshly-dug grave and tell yourself your feet are not closer to the edge of that void than they ought to be." Veece cracked a smile.

"And you're off again with *the void*. Know what, I noticed something about you. Ye only ever smile when you're talking about the graves. Think that's normal, do ya?"

"We will be put in our own soon enough. We may want to get comfortable with the idea of being there for eternity."

"You need to stop talking about eternity, and the void and the *shroud of dusk*, Veece. People will think you mad. God knows the thought has crossed my mind," Monte said. He took a bite of the apple he'd been polishing on his hempen cowl. It was a sad piece of fruit, somewhat shriveled and dotted with bruises.

"Drop the seed of an apple into a grave and see what fruit is yielded," Veece said.

"Aye then. I just might."

"Look. The chimney above has nearly bisected the moon. Time draws near."

Monte took a few bites of his apple before answering. "I'm ready to go now. Let's be done with this foul business."

"No," Veece said with iron in his usually soft voice. "I won't be caught bodysnatching. You know the punishment. Though I suspect soon medicine will advance in such a way that corpses will be used freely, we don't have that luxury now, on this very night. We wait."

Monte ate every last bite of his apple, including the core, and ignored his partner's comment. They watched as two torch-bearing men with rifles walked by the alley's mouth without so much as glancing at the shadows within.

"We go now," Veece said and slipped away from the wall he had been leaning upon. Monte grabbed both shovels and followed.

Boston was enduring a harsh winter and on that night it was too cold for snow. It would make the digging hard, laborious work. They edged their way north into town, crossing block after block of closed businesses and homes with darkened stoops and pulled drapes. The salty stink of the sea and fishing vessels wafted across the city.

The nineteenth century had just begun three years previous, and the buildings were being built constantly taller. Dwellings had grown like barnacles. Bricks rose and arched along city squares, across the harbors, as far as the eye could see. Nightlife had formed in the cracks of a new society, birthed in the shadows despite guard patrols and the revealing light of torches. Other night marauders were occasionally seen sneaking along the rows of riverside homes and across streets lined with warehouses, off to do their own master's bidding, whoever that may be and whether or not that was a governor with the coin for medical experiments concerning cadavers.

"There's talk of putting in more graves, you know," Monte said when they had gotten far enough down Hull street to see the Copp's Hill Burial Ground. "More and more folks are dying--

acres of graveyard planned, I hear. Shame we can't pluck who we please."

"Our doctor is particular, you're not wrong. Keep your eyes on the grounds."

Copp's Hill was cloaked in frost and shadow. Ahead, silhouetted against the pale night sky, tombstones both crude and opulent could be seen jutting up from the ground behind the thick wrought iron fence. Clutters of stone and marble tickled the skyline on a smooth curve of hill in the form of tombs and obelisks, constructs of all shapes and likenesses.

Veece and Monte hid in a stairwell across the street, leading to a basement. Looking up at the graveyard, they could spot the newly-constructed guard house. Half a watchtower, half a hovel, the mortar-and-stone building housed the night watch over the cemetery grounds. Too many corpses had been exhumed as of late, the business of bodysnatching alive and thriving in the bowels of medicine's advancing industry.

"The rifleman is inside, probably warming his hands. It's too cold for lookout tonight," Veece said.

Monte was trying to keep from chattering his teeth and failing. "G-go! H-hurry it up."

Veece shook his head. "No. Wait for a guard to peer out of the bow loop."

"Stop telling me no Veece. It's too damn c-cold for caution tonight."

Veece had his eyes closed. "Peculiar, more like." "Huh?"

"The doctor, he is peculiar more than particular." "Ye and you along with him. Speak your head, man." Veece opened his eyes and looked toward the gates of the cemetery. "The men we have been exhuming, they aren't for medical research, Monte. I've spent afternoons at the Historical Society in addition to City Hall.

There are papers saved there, names writ upon them. Each and every man we have snatched from the earth bores a singular purpose. I just don't know what it is yet."

Monte threw his large, calloused hands into the air. "You and yer books, Veece. Always with the names of long-dead men and their deeds." That barb was not sharp coming from an illiterate man.

"The corpses are from Salem, Monte. Not directly, not all of them, but descended from that place, yes."

"Never been t' Salem, me. Don't see what a place like that means for a man like me."

"What then, does Salem mean to the good doctor?"

"Dunno, I prob'ly won't be one to figure it. If yer standing here waiting t' hear my piece, well, dawn's around the corner."

Veece exited the stairway and strode quickly to a more furtive section of fencing. He climbed, Monte after him, both in silence. They walked and weaved between stone markers and mausoleums, Veece reading by moonlight as they went.

"Here," Veece said, coming to a ruddy stone marker set against the back of a mortared wall. "The grave of one Barnabas Curwen." It read:

Barnabas Curwen
Borne 1622 - Diede 1692

"This is perplexing," Veece said, staring at the writing chiseled into the tombstone. He explained to Monte, "The man has been dead more than a century. What use is this to a doctor?"

Monte shrugged. "What about the others we got out of the ground? They looked fresh enough."

"Deceased recently. Grandchildren of these men, perhaps. Though why the good doctor wants to dig into another era, I do not know."

Monte nodded with an impatient air. "No point in freezing our balls off out here." He grabbed a shovel and drove it down into the hard-packed earth. Winter had solidified the ground to a nearly brick-like quality. As the night wore on and their shovels dug deeper into the grave of a mysterious man, the sweat and grime of their efforts worked heat into their limbs.

Veece kept stealing glances at the gravestone's written remembrance of a man. He looked back through his memory to what he'd read about Salem and their witch trials. Young women had begun to contort into unlikely forms and speak the name of ancient demons. The Puritan hammer fell quickly with devastating weight. Twenty people were tortured and killed during a torrent of hysteria in which the evidence was all but spectral.

Crude tests were implanted to secure the fate of the mostly-female suspects of witchcraft. The accused swiftly condemned innocents to save themselves from being burned alive or flayed. Veece had read about the Witch Cake, made by one of the minister's slaves. The cake had been comprised of rye meal and the urine of each supposedly afflicted girl. The Witch Cake was then fed to a dog which in turn would cause suffering to the leader of the coven, thus revealing her.

It had failed along with the Touch Tests in Andover. Women desperately lied in hopes for safety.

It was understood that esoteric, forbidden texts were being used in Salem Town, Salem Village, Ispwich, and Andover to communicate with obscure magicks and those beings with no name. The tongues thus spoke were removed, silenced forever.

The good doctor wanted to hear what they had said perhaps, or it could be that he wanted to peer into an arcane vista of knowledge beyond that of Christian Science.

It took hours to completely dig down to the crude pine box. With three strong stabs of a shovel, Veece was able to pry open the thin lid of the coffin. It was too cold for rot, but the body looked as if it had never decayed at all. "The flesh, it's coarse," Veece said, having reached down to touch the strange, loosely-knit skin upon old bones.

"Coarse or not, get 'im in the bag. C'mon. Quick now." Veece said nothing from within the pit. He pulled back large splinters of wood and pried at the lid until the cadaver was entirely visible. Once a man, the body looked to have died young despite its supposed seven-decade life. Dressed in a plain wool spun shift, it was possible to see his bones in places but not many.

"Veece?" Monte called down as softly as he could manage. "You down there reading or somethin'?"

"The body is too large for the sack, and in too-good of shape anyway." Veece rummaged around inside his hempen garb, grabbing a burlap sack he had strapped to his leg with a cord of leather. "Break his neck and feet and we go."

Monte nodded. He crawled down into the grave. "Go topside and let me do my work, then."

Veece did. He heard the sounds of sinew and bone parting. Grunts and curses rose from the grave as Monte made the necessary adjustments. Minutes later two large filthy hands gripped the edge of the grave and Monte pulled himself out, panting.

"He's all yours." Monte clapped a gloved hand on the other man's shoulder.

Veece saw the corpse's head lolling to one side in an unnatural position. The feet were both angled straight down, dangling away from the ankles. It took some maneuvering to get the body out of the coffin and into the burlap sack but Veece managed, cinching tight the leather cord at the top to secure their work.

All the while Veece thought about how it looked like they were stealing a living man from the earth. He wanted to ask Monte if he thought the witches truly had ever obtained any magic but decided against it.

Veece began to shovel dirt from the mounds around the gravestone back into the grave. Monte could not help but chuckle. "Really? With all that's goin' on in cemeteries at night we are the two men who fill the grave back up?"

"Well, you aren't one of those men. You just happen to be accompanying one such. Let me get back to work. Go bring it back to the good doctor if you want. I'll be along shortly."

"Ye know what? Ye…" Monte started and let his voice fall away. "Aye, a'right then, Veece. Shovel ice and dirt if you want, I'm gonna take your advice for once and go back t' town. Maybe I can still find a woman at the tavern, if all the tight ones haven't been taken at this hour, that is. I know the rum will be there for me either way and so I'll be pissed until morn!"

Veece answered only by shoveling.

Monte was gone without another word.

Veece finished after a long while, feeling exhilarated and exhausted by the hard work. He wouldn't forget the crudely-carved inscription on that tombstone. Especially what had been written below the dashed numbers that encapsulated the man's existence.

Barnabas Curwen

***

Veece reached his destination before dawn. The city of Boston was coming alive. Already on the streets men and women were bustling about or transporting carriages filled with all manner of goods from the land, the sea, and across the world old and new.

It would be his final day in Boston. The last two transactions with the doctor had been bizarre and disturbing to say the least. Yes, it was time to move on with what money he could manage lest he end up like those witches in Salem.

Further south by the lower ports, in a trash-strewn alley with a floor matted in decomposed organic matter, Veece arrived at a weathered set of wooden doors secured to the top of a basement staircase. Looking first left, then right for any watching passersby, he produced a key from his pocket and unlocked the brass handle of the cellar door. Once opened, the door belched a foul odor.

"Veece," a voice said behind him. "I decided to wait on that woman. The rum too, aye. We have t' talk."

Veece let the handmade dagger in his right sleeve slide down into his palm. He turned to regard Monte. The man looked haggard in the morning light, beyond that of a tired and cold and horny man, as if all the rum in the world had attacked him and left him barely living.

"The doctor didn't pay me. Said... well, he said he won't speak. What's that supposed t' mean? I ask him, who, who don't speak? Mad bastard pointed at the corpse!"

"His mind is slipping. The good doctor's sanity is frayed farther than the hemp of your cowl Monte."

"Was gonna buy a new one with my money. Can't now though, can I?" What Monte was not asking Veece was *what are we going to do about it?*

"You go out and get yourself a shave and some new clothes and get out of town. That's what you can do," Veece said. He descended the grimy steps into the cellar.

Monte followed. "If yer gonna kill the man, ye may as well just run now. The governor's coin travels faster than ye do. Aye ye know that. This ain't about *medicine*--the things we've got for him. Even with the wits God gave me that's plain t' see."

"And how fast will his master's coin put men on my heels if I don't return to the doctor for my money? My absence would appear suspicious. I seek to conclude this now in the morning rather than the middle of tonight with a dagger at my throat.

"You were right about one thing, Monte: our work has nothing to do with the academic pursuit of human anatomy. It's about coin, and that coin is being withheld."

Monte gestured downward, toward the iron-banded door at the end of a short, wet hallway made of stone. Veece strode to open the door, entering the work space of Doctor Thelton.

Piles of books and leather-bound tomes were scattered along the entryway, forcing the door to a premature stop. The two men navigated through a pathway of junk, books and crates, taking a left into a circular room like that of an amphitheater.

Rather than people seated in the auditorium the good doctor had ordered built, leaning towers of moldy texts surrounded the central floor where he worked alongside alchemy tools of sizes both miniature and extraordinary. A hand-carved oak desk sat situated on the right side of the circular floor, opposite a row of metal tables covered in sheets. Dirty orange stains speckled the otherwise white cloth.

"Please, advance toward my desk," the doctor said. "Do not be coy, after the gravework has already been done. It is warm in here, as hospitable an environment as any to have a conversation. Come Veece, let me hear what you have to say."

The silver chandelier chained to the apex of the rotund ceiling provided dim, flickering candlelight. Veece stood in the ring of light, centered in front of Doctor Thelton's desk. Sheaves of paperwork cluttered the oak top, hardly any of it written in English. The man wore oval-shaped glasses and kept what little wiry hair was left on the sides of his head.

"Well? What do you have to say for yourself, Veece? Come, take down your hood and explain to me the art of your failure." Veece did not move or respond, only stared the doctor in his small, beady eyes. "Yes, well, men as learned as I do not have the luxury of time so I will have our conversation. Join in any time you like." Monte shifted behind Veece, switching his considerable weight from one foot to the other. He spared glances at the doctor, but none connecting eye contact. "The two of you brought me a specimen outside the parameters of my request. Not in flesh but in form, which one eventually comes to envision as singular. I cannot fathom that my instructions could be misinterpreted. Verbatim, I told you both that he needed to speak! I want to know about Joseph Curwen, but you must have done something to ruin the connection, yes, the two of you somehow interrupted a dweomer constructed in the seventeenth century, yes that must be it-- sheer, raw ignorance-"

"What's wrong with the body?" Veece asked. He was standing still as stone, the perfect imitation of the good doctor's many medical mannequins. Doctor Thelton had never expressed a desire for the body to *speak* to the gravediggers, but rather had been secretive and vague about his purposes. Veece had never heard the name Curwen until reading it on a gravestone the previous evening.

"You know exactly what was wrong with the body you-you butcher! You slaughterer!" the doctor said, throwing down the leather bound book he'd been holding open onto his desk. "It will not do! I repeated the verses-- I read them all correctly on the right dates, you see. I performed to the letter and now *nothing!* I waited, oh how I waited! Each Roodmas and every Hallow's Eve, I spake the verses, I waited for it to breed in the outside spheres.

"What did I receive pro quo? *Silence! You two* have cast a shadow of failure upon my work. What other explanation is there? Surely you do not deign to suggest I have misinterpreted the book? Surely the shadow of ignorance has not led you so severely astray?"

"Give me the money I am owed and I will become the very image of a shadow," Veece said. "We never agreed to dead man's words and I've no taste for the madness you speak of."

"Monte, do you want to step forward and say the same?" The doctor gently removed his spectacles and placed them on his desk, one leg crossed atop the other and his hands folded comfortably in his lap. "Hmm? I cannot hear the two of you what with the timidity. I cannot hear anything at all, no. Not from my specimen certainly."

Veece again let slip the dagger in his sleeve, holding it openly now. It was plain but sharpened professionally.

Monte grabbed Veece's arm. "The governor won't like this, Veece. Let's get going. Forget the money."

"Fools. Incomprehensible morons! Things may have begun to breed and here you sit speaking of *money.* Regardless of the failure in flesh you presented me, I know what the book has said." The good doctor wore a peevish smile. "I've heard the others speak to me--oh yes. Those from Salem before my current lifetime, those that spake of a true god, an ageless one larger than our collective perception. He has been sleeping. He has been asleep a long, long time. Dreaming his dreams of rotting meat."

The doctor kept his eyes on the knife, watching it calmly. He looked amused, wholly mad.

"You cannot kill me. No, not truly," Doctor Thelton said as simply as if discussing the weather. His tone had mellowed in an extreme manner. He grabbed an odd book from a teetering stack on the floor beside him. Its cover was scarred by whorls of discoloration and unfair textures. "Flay the flesh from me and I still will not speak to you, not if you spent tenfold the lifetimes I have devoted to this work! Pour your soul into the pages of obscurity like so many before me! Hear loud the silence!"

"The coin owed," Veece screamed. He stabbed the dagger into the thick oak slab of desk in front of him, skewering a sheaf of papers.

"Not even the gods fight necessity," Doctor Thelton said in a dry voice he had not been using moments ago. "Will you Monte? Veece the Infallible is set against a perpetual disaster course throughout the infinite cosmos, but you? Is your ineptitude greater than I imagined?"

Monte handed Veece the shovel he'd carried in with him. "Sorry, doc. Don't even know what that all means, really."

"Ah. The book here in my hands has shown me things I cannot describe in any language written by man. It has shown that you will kill me with a shovel in a small-moment's time. It has shown me that you have done so a thousand-thousand times before, in a repetition I have freed myself from at last. Did you know this is not Barnabas Curwen beneath this sheet? Afflicted by magicks, surely, though not a true Curwen.

"Did you know you are but a dream once had by a long-dead god? You are not real. You cannot kill m-"

Veece swung the shovel sideways. It cut into Doctor Thelton's head, ripping loose a large flap of skin. The resounding thud had a gristly tint to it. The blow had sent the doctor sprawling out of his chair to land awkwardly among a pile of books and papers.

The mad man was laughing, holding the rent skin of his head in place with a trembling hand. "I know nothing! Killing me won't change the truth of my work --go ahead and read it for yourself. Find out how little you know! In knowledge ignorance teems! You too will realize what it means to have heard the corpses speak!"

With a crooked finger the doctor pointed at the tome bound in a patchwork of unknown material. It had fallen open on the desk.

"Gaze upon the abyss, Veece. May your learning undo what you know."

Standing above the good doctor, Veece lowered the shovel. He pressed it against the soft skin of the man's cheek and stepped heavily onto the foot rest.

Eventually the gurgling noises ended and the doctor's feet stopped kicking against the cool stone ground.

"Well now what?" Monte asked. The candles in the chamber had burned down lower, partially masking his face. "Had ye thought this through before dealing with Shovelhead there?"

Veece watched as the crimson stain spread out over parchments, seeping across the grouting like mortar to the stones beneath. He knew that the building had been founded that way, on blood and secrets.

"We bury him in Curwen's grave. Tonight." "Who in the Hell is Curwen?"

Veece leaned the shovel against the oak desk and sat in the leather chair. "It doesn't matter anymore," he replied, having peered at the open book the late doctor had spoken of. "Let's leave the wretched book here. I don't think minds like ours can entertain the diseased fancies within its pages. We will burn his entire sanctum."

"Yer the boss," Monte said. "Let's meet back here tonight and finish this business. We will go our separate ways after that, aye. I don't like what I saw here tonight."

Veece didn't reply or look up from the book. He was already turning its vellum pages.

***

That evening, Monte's internal alarm awoke him. It was midnight, the bloated and pale moon scarfed by a scrim of thin clouds. As good a night as any to leave a life in Boston behind. He'd slept in an alleyway, half-standing in a hunch. If the governor's men were to wake him, he had to be ready. But they didn't, and he had wondered if the governor himself didn't know the location of Doctor Thelton's study.

Maybe there were more hidden throughout the city.

Monte hurried through the night, twice walking in the wrong direction only to backtrack and look for any followers. None were out. The night was the coldest yet this season, a snap of frost that was fierce enough to outright kill a man of lesser constitution.

The cellar door was still unlocked when Monte finally made it, though he couldn't feel the iron on his fingers because they had gone numb with cold even through his gloves.

No matter how numb his nose had gotten beneath his threadbare cowl, Monte knew the smell which clotted the

27

entryway, a smell he had grown to know intimately in the war: the decay of human flesh. Like his ma's venison stew, there was nothing else like it in the world and once the scent hit your nose so too did the certainty that soup was on.

Monte shut the door behind him and hopped down the short stone stairs, glad for the warmer atmosphere and wanting a bowl of chunky venison stew. He pawed the iron-banded door open and stifled a response to the corpse rot. It was possibly the worst he'd ever smelled, even when cleaning up after amputations some years ago when the battles had finished.

Around the towering, esoteric items, Monte walked into the dark hall. "Veece… what have you done?" he asked.

Spread across the floor in a circular shape, connected by a spider web of sinew, lay the limbs, genitals and head of Doctor Thelton. Each had been bundled and bound by viscera with care and precision, wound together with the next separated lump of flesh to create an atrocious image like writing. Veece crouched in the center of the obscenity, reading aloud from the book he had apparently been unable to put down.

"Plikk-pa-na-kk'i-kkla jin-ka-ielll'ea jke-a jke-a."

"No. No, no, *no, no, no,*" Monte said. "I… I can understand ye. I know them words. Somehow I know 'em!"

Of Veece's right hand, little remained. It looked like he had chewed three fingers to the bone and bitten through his thumb entirely. Grisly, ragged wounds had been ground into the pages, inking the book in blood.

It looked as if the vellum of an alien creature drank the fluids, writing the strange scripture with his lifeforce.

Insane ramblings continued to pour from Veece's mouth, spilling from his chewed lips and through cracked teeth. His speech pattern was lilting, quick and fragmented. Long, roped tatters of his lips clung to his chin, showing his bloodied teeth. It looked like he had bitten off his tongue as well.

The shovel was still leaning against the oak desk.

Monte ran to it and held it as tightly as he could. He threw all the might of his body into the swing, landing the shovel directly into Veece's head.

The tortured sound of his hoarse voice did not cease, but rather took on a new life. It sounded like two other people were speaking from Veece's mouth.

Monte swung again, and once more. His strength frenzied then, urged forward by his own fear. It felt to him like there was another man in the room, the way you know when someone is watching. Veece had left something behind when he read the book and the only way Monte knew to deal with it was to keep chopping with the shovel until it went away. He could feel the eyes on his back, all around him. Thousands of eyes, peering from far away.

It was grim work removing the head but it was done, persuaded by a faint voice he couldn't understand, did not want to understand.

A whisper seemed to linger in the air, beneath his skull, repeating something. It was very like his own voice.

One borne who shal looke Backe.

A cold sweat had cropped up on Monte's hairy arms during the labor. He felt he needed to sit despite the hot, pressing smell. The voice had left his head in loud silence. A thought occurred.

What was in the book?

He decided it would be best to immediately bury the tome in the empty grave of the Curwen man. But then he wondered again at its contents.

In the end, he was unable to find a cure for his curiosity. Monte opened it. Its pages gazed back, watchful as a human eye.

It looked like the crusted scab of bloodied words was moving, writhing ever so slightly off the page like maggots.

Strange, for an illiterate man to sit and read a book, but there he was. This one he could understand somehow.

***

In 1815 a man named William Mathers purchased a long-abandoned building near the bustling ports and wharfs of Boston. It had been an exciting find, what with no previous owner standing to contest the price whatsoever. It had been as if the bank wanted excessively to be rid of the massive estate.

William arrived by ship on the 1st of February 1815, directing the few men in his employ to unload what belongings he had sailed with into his newly acquired abode.

He told the men he'd have himself a look around to see what kind of deal he had really struck upon.

A bit cavernous, the building was stout rather than tall. It would require some considerate decorating to entirely furnish the two gigantic rooms which comprised his new home, not to mention the singular room set off from what William considered the main belly of the place. A bedroom in an odd location is not so bad a bargain. Within it he found naught but a tattered, moth-eaten rug on the floor and an empty shipping crate.

It took two days to clean the building and place his furniture in meaningful positions. The second evening, William almost laughed out loud despite his exhaustion: they'd finished their labors but forgotten the rug in his small bedroom. Such a time-eaten thing did not belong among his polished antiquities and fine furniture.

Pulled away, the rug revealed a trap door that puzzled William to no end. The paperwork had included no information about a basement or subterranean space. If it had been neglected, all the better. It was his fortune to find without cost.

The thick brass ring on the latch would not lift. Puzzlement furthered William's sore feet. He checked high and low inside his new home and found no means for exit or entry into another, lower space.

The exterior of the building yielded little else until he searched in the alley behind. Previously, throughout the last two days, he had espied the stone entrance to what appeared to be a cistern of city property or that of his neighbor. A planked wooden door was set into the face of the stone construct and not a thought one had occurred toward the breaking and entering of the squat addition.

Now William knew for a certainty that it led into the bowels of his own building and had not been created by the city or a business, but was his and his alone to delve into.

How easily the weak, rotted wood of its door lifted away from the hinges!

A cloying stink rose from the yawning little stairway. Wet stone and mildew offended his nose as he descended, and when he opened another door set at the bottom of the short stairwell, realized the stone was stained by the scent of something else. Chemicals, he was fairly sure, though he'd never been around any abundantly.

William struck a match and ventured further by the light of a brass lantern. Inside a short hallway the miasma intensified, the smell becoming appalling. Trash and junk was strewn across the path and piled along the cobbled walkway, all manner of instruments both glass and metal, wooden remnants of human-like figures and furniture now broken.

The passageway opened into a room very like a cistern: round and cold, created more for purpose than decorum. The smell was forgotten as he looked around at what had been left behind in the strange place. More instruments of peculiar and somewhat sinister design, along with stacks of books and moldering sheaves of paper.

William rifled through the books at his feet, not able to understand the language any were written in. The titles were entirely foreign to him.

At last he made his way toward the back of the room and approached an oak desk. He would have liked such a handsome slab of wood had it not been penetrated so fully by the smell of the place. It bore a long, scarring gouge across its face.

The first desk drawer was stuffed full of rambling gibberish written on parchment paper. Page after page showed diagrams and illustrations and even what looked like the practice of handwriting.

William noticed how the hand had begun to write so crudely, with hardly a grasp on the alphabet, but after pages were turned, began to sharpen and collect an experienced stroke. Eventually, toward the back of the nonsense text, he came to see the sawing, crabbed hand of a man no longer communicating in English from any nearby century.

The second drawer was empty besides an envelope. Inside was a short, unsent letter, one that would mystify William Mather until his dying day.

Who had owned the building before, or what their purpose was within that obscure laboratory, never revealed itself to William. It was only clear that there had at one time been a book studied beneath the floors of his home and the men whom were researching it cared very dearly to see it understood.

From where those men had come, to where they fled, and their baffling suggestion of being an ancient age, were questions burning hotly in William Mather until his untimely end on a venture at sea.

The secret of the letter's existence died with him and was never read again.

***

My Antient ffriende--

My waite for my com'g Backe is come. Wordes and Stepps to bringe up YOGGE-SOTHOTHE haue Readied his Hande, and here I will owne no knowledge of Heir or Saltes, nor ye Tryalls you Knowe.

ye Thing breedes in ye Outside Spheres. Honour'd Brother, I am yr true ffriende and Servt. For the Bookes you haue Hadd Sup'lied to Docttor Theltone haue made me an Other fromm Saltes unknown. The Booke needes tyme, even wiith What we Knowe. A Specimen of Theltone was call'd up but yt was not Barnabas Curwen, and knew lesse about the Outside. I suspect his Stone was chang'd at the groundes.

I am in a sorry state to ask, but firste I neede these texts as followes: the Artephius' Key of Wisdom, Ars Magna et Ultima, the Necronomicon (as withe aall works and Wordes of Abdul Alhazred), and the booke of Borellus.

Yf these Wordes are not receiv'd, I will write agin. There are Sailors who would knowe my fface ffor surely the featu'es of this man haue changed, and my Seat may neede to alter too.

Send the items to a One Monte Allen, 23 Hull Street, Boston, MA. I have been call'd up Out of Space to read ye Booke of No Name, ffor one hundred more yeares if need'd. I hope I may see you not longe ffrom now, in this lif'time.

Brother in Almousin-Metraton,

The End.

CASE #90738

BREEDING IN THE SPHERES
BY TYLER TRISTAO

Born and raised in western Washington State, I grew up enjoying rainy days spent inside reading. The written worlds of Stephen King, George R.R. Martin, and Chuck Palahniuk inspired me to craft my own. On dark, grey days I write noir, horror and fantasy.

I am a novelist and creator of short stories.

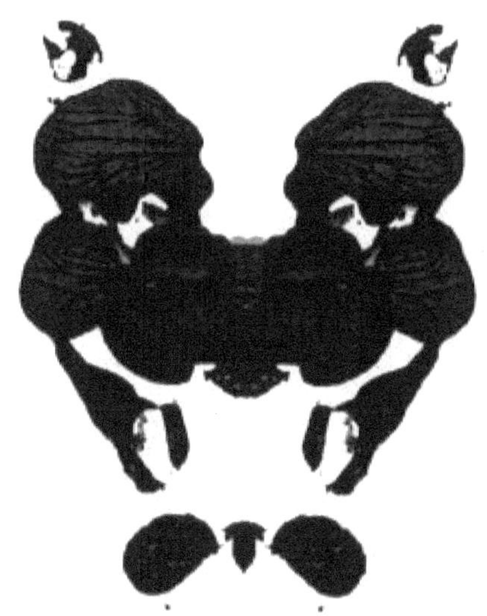

The Journal of the Median Man – A Face on the Wall by Barry Price

I had been walking along the forest path for about an hour when I heard the deep growl of thunder behind me. I stopped and looked back down the trail, leaning on my longrifle. Bright shafts of late afternoon sunlight slanted down through the canopy of leaves and played over the forest floor like sunbeams in a tropical lagoon, dancing in an ever-shifting mosaic of radiant yellow and green patches. The sparkling vision brought to mind a famous Lakota saying: "Beauty before me, beauty behind me, beauty above me, and beauty below me - in beauty I walk."

It was a clear, hot July day; hushed and oppressively humid, even in the deep shade of the woods. I was somewhere northwest of Harper's Ferry, about ten miles from the nearest highway, exploring a newly established historical park tucked away up in the hills. The original settlement was founded in the1750's, and enjoyed modest growth for the next hundred years. Then Confederate raiders swept through the area in 1864, a few days in advance of the battle at Gettysburg, and the inhabitants fled to the surrounding countryside, never to return. There wasn't much of the little hamlet left now; just a few houses, barns, and tumbled stone foundations. But what remained was in a remarkably good state of preservation, and since I was passing through the area anyway, I thought I'd give it a look.

A sudden chill wind pungent with the smell of rain gusted through the forest, sending showers of leaves fluttering down from the canopy. In the distance, a tall, black cumulo-nimbus cloud loomed on the western horizon, sweeping over the hills like a tidal wave. I propped the rifle against a tree and pulled open the front of my hunting frock, letting the breeze cool my sweating limbs.

I was just drinking in the vast, green smell of the summer woods when a flash of lightning cracked down into the ridge about a half-mile away. Two seconds later, thunder boomed though the trees, driving gaggles of birds flapping and squawking into the woods.

The storm was getting closer, the sky quickly darkening overhead.

I checked my pocket-watch...about three in the afternoon. I reckoned the storm would be here in twenty minutes, maybe sooner. No time to put up my oilcloth lean-to; I'd have to find shelter right now. I scanned the tourist map I had found earlier, and it looked like one of the remaining intact stone houses was about a mile up ahead. I figured it would take me about ten minutes to get to the place, if I jogged all the way. There being nothing else for it, I cinched up my gear, slung my rifle, and took off down the trail.

The woodland path ahead of me was still brightly sunlit, and I made good speed as I hustled along, up hills and down hollows. Then I rounded a blind corner and ran up on a shallow creek rushing across the path. It was too broad to leap or pole-vault over, so I had to wade across barefoot, first removing my shoe-pack moccasins and stuffing them under my sash. Even in the middle of a very hot summer day, the water was icy cold, and my feet were blue and numb by the time I got to the other side. I was just slipping the moccasins back on and lashing the leggings down over them when the first fat drops of rain began to slap down through the leaves. I strapped my greased cow's-knee over the flintlock, then bolted down the path at a dead run.

I had just cleared the trees and run out into an open field when there was another flash of lightning off to my right. Instantly, a heavy shock-wave of thunder pounded across the field, almost blowing me off my feet. Then the sky opened, and the rain came beating down onto the forest like a million tons of buckshot. It looked like I was going to get a thorough soaking, and hypothermia into the bargain.

But then, up ahead, the stone building I was looking for appeared just off the path to my left, nestled in a stand of ancient red maples. I put on a final burst of speed, and a few more strides took me under the trees and out of the heaviest downpour. The house was a few dozen yards farther ahead at the end of a tumbled flagstone path, and I had to pick my way carefully over the muddy, slippery, upturned rocks to avoid turning my ankles. After a few stumbling near-spills, I hopped up onto the front stoop and under the eaves of the building.

I pressed back against the stone wall and took a quick look around. The churning blackness of the storm was directly overhead now; rain crashing down through the forest with such a deafening roar that the noise wiped out every other sound but the crack and boom of thunder. Water was pouring down off the slate roof like Niagara, excavating a shallow moat around the building. It was time to get inside.

I tried the front door. It wouldn't budge...probably nailed shut. I ran around to the back of the building, and found what I hoped would be there; a sloping potato-cellar hatch close up against the wall. I seized the twin doors and pulled them open, wafting a cloud of clammy, dirt-smelling air up into my face. I stepped down the uneven granite slabs and into the dank, subterranean vault. Then I turned and let the doors fall shut, plunging the low dirt cellar into blackness.

I stood absolutely still for a moment, listening. Close to hand, runoff from the eaves splattered down on the hatch and trickled over the rough granite steps onto the floor. In the distance, I could hear trees in the surrounding forest groaning, splintering, and crashing to the ground as the storm raged with growing intensity. It was one of those moments when nature presents such a terrible and alien aspect that one can only retreat from it.

Happily, I was out of the storm and safe indoors. Or so I thought. I pulled out my flashlight and played the beam over the thick strata of mist that floated motionless in the stagnant air. The cellar smelled very strongly of damp soil, moldy potatoes, wood smoke, and soft coal. For a country boy like me, it was a comfortable, homey kind of a smell.

But homey or not, I needed to get upstairs and out of this stuffy crypt. I swept the flashlight beam around in a search for a way up, and sure enough, there was a plank staircase fixed to the wall at the far end of the cellar. It was steep and narrow, like a ship's companionway, and probably way too rickety to bear any weight at all. I crouched down and shuffled carefully across the lumpy earthen floor, roiling the mist into ominous, staring vortexes. As I got to the stair, I gave it a tentative shake. To my surprise, it was unmoving and solid as a rock. I stepped up onto the planks and climbed to the main room.

The door to the ground floor was the standard article – made of solid black oak, six feet tall, three feet wide, complete with marble doorknob, latch, and keyhole. But instead of being built into the wall, it was hinged on the floor, like a trapdoor. I took a few more steps up the stair, then pressed my hands against the door and gave it a hard push. It swung open and away, slamming the knob against the floor with a loud bang and sending a thick cloud of gritty dust billowing into the air. I climbed up into the pitch-dark room.

Flashes of lightning blinked through the boarded-over windows, illuminating the blind dark with quick flashgun bursts.

Deep thunder rolled across the fields and through the ground, rattling the house like a giant kettle-drum.

I moved away from the cellar stair and swung the light beam over the floor. It was made of the wavy, adze-cut oaken planks common to the period, blanketed with a woolly sediment of dust. Wider scrutiny revealed a layer of sparkling glass shards near the windows, with the rest of the room strewn with chunks of ceiling plaster, wallpaper scraps, and other random debris that crunched and crackled underfoot as I walked. I moved out into the middle of the floor and played the light around the walls. Most of the indigo-pattern wallpaper had long since peeled away and lay on the floor in moldy, curled-up cylinders. The bare plaster walls were heavily water-stained, sagging, and in places crumbled away to expose coarse, sandy under-plaster and splintered lathing.

I was just moving the beam to the section over the central fireplace when a terrific flash of lightning lit up the room, followed by an explosion like an Earthquake Bomb that knocked me off my feet. As I went down, the flashlight bounced out of my hand and went clattering across the floor, coming to rest on a mound of crumbled plaster a few feet away. I dusted myself off and walked over to retrieve the flashlight. As I stooped to pick it up, I noticed that the light was aimed at an unusual water stain just over the fireplace. I picked up the flashlight and, keeping the beam centered on the stain, I approached the wall for a better look. As I got closer, the rust-tinted blotch began to resolve into what looked like the face of a young girl.

Now, it's a well-known quirk of the human mind to read faces into water-stains, rocks, clouds, and other nebulous shapes; but this was no accidental pattern of discolorations. It was a very precisely defined and haunting image of a young girl in the throes of some terrible sadness and grief.

I turned the light away from the wall, hoping that fatigue, shock, and the tempest wailing outside had caused me to imagine something that wasn't there. After a few seconds, I turned the beam back on the wall, hoping to see just a vague arrangement of splotches that kind of looked like a face.

But no. The same melancholy image was still there, and it seemed to be coalescing into sharper definition as I looked at it. Worse, it now appeared to be turning its gaze directly towards me. I flicked off the light and backed away from the wall.

This ain't happening, I thought. I couldn't have just seen that.

Because if I *did* just see that, then there were only two possible explanations for it: either this Godforsaken place is haunted, or I'm losing my bloody mind. I didn't find either prospect attractive, and under normal circumstances I would just turn and head for the exit, molto rapido.

But there was this big, violent storm raging outside; one of the worst I'd ever seen, and I was out in the middle of nowhere West Virginia - ten miles away from anything at all. Not to mention that it was darker than Satan's butt-hole outside. Well…except for the constant fusillades of lightning cracking down from the sky like incoming artillery. So it looked like I would be spending the night here in this house - haunted or not, crazy or not.

Calmer now, I approached the wall once again and slowly moved the beam onto the ghostly visage. As I fixed the light on it, the thing suddenly turned to look at me, staring directly into my soul. I gasped and staggered backwards, averting my eyes from the face that now gazed upon me with the force of a living presence.

Well, I thought…haunted it is, then. No question of that now, even if I *was* losing my bloody mind. And that might be in the cards, too, if I dared to spend the night here.

But what the hell else was I gonna do? I could always flee, of course, but I would almost certainly perish in the storm; either from hypothermia, or in some stupid, random accident - like a bloody, bone-cracking fall into an unseen gorge full of jagged boulders.

Or, I could stay and risk my sanity, and maybe my life. But…maybe there was a third choice here: Maybe I could acknowledge this lost soul trying to communicate with me…invite her to tell me her story. And since I was trapped in this disturbed house until morning, it seemed like the only thing left to do. So, reluctantly, fighting every instinct of mind and body, I turned back to the image on the wall and locked eyes with the entity. A cold shock jolted my body, and I began to tremble violently, like a high-voltage current was pulsing through me. But the shock and trembling subsided, and I was able to keep my eyes steady on the image. I settled my mind, remembering that the spirits are with us at all times, and are generally not to be feared. All they want, mostly, is the simple acknowledgment that they are there.

Holding firmly to this conviction, I moved to within a few feet of the image and, opening my mind to the spirit, I invited it to declare its mind. The face began to move its lips, as if it were trying to form words. I could detect no audible sound, especially over the savage howling of the storm, but as I bent my concentration to its utmost, I began to receive… not the fear, horror, or threat that I expected; but instead, a terrible sense of desolation, grief, and unbearable loneliness. I averted my eyes again, breaking off the connection rather than endure one more instant of the searing anguish that was flowing from the wraith. After a few moments, I shook my head and returned my gaze to the apparition.

But the image was suddenly frozen, staring into the darkness like a blind thing. I tried to re-establish contact, but the apparition had gone mute, the spirit departed, and the sense of dread I felt a few seconds before faded away. My awareness slowly returned to the present, and I was conscious again of the rain slapping against the walls and the wind moaning around the eaves.

I switched off the flashlight and slumped down to the floor. I was feeling very wobbly from hunger and emotional strain, and I needed a hot meal and a night's sleep. There was a large kitchen-fireplace in the front wall, but I had no idea if it was safe to use.

I rolled over to the hearth and aimed the flashlight up the chimney. The wind outside shrieked across the chimney-top, causing little showers of dirt to filter down the shaft into my face. I pulled my hat over my eyes until the particles stopped falling, then continued my inspection. As far up as I could see there were no obstructions; no branches, leaves, squirrel or bird nests clogging the flue. I couldn't see all the way up to the top because the shaft took a dogleg near the top to divert rainwater down a separate rain-channel. But the central chimney was clear.

Good. I could have myself a hot meal tonight, then a cozy chimney-corner to curl up and have a smoke afterwards. And then a good night's sleep.

Next thing would be to find some dry firewood. Luckily, somebody, (probably one of the restoration crews), had left some partially burned logs on the hearth-grate and, better still, a neatly stacked pile of split locust wood in the chimney-corner; more than enough to see me through the night. I laid my knapsack on the floor and started setting up for dinner.

I got a little cook-fire going, then knocked together my standard dinner of beans, cornmeal and bacon. The large fireplace was equipped with several cast-iron swivel-arms, enabling me to hang my little tin cook-pot over the flames right away. Next, I crushed up some coffee beans, tossed them in my coffee boiler, and hung it over the fire next to the already bubbling cook-pot. Ten minutes later, dinner was served.

Outside, the storm had settled into a steady, all-night downpour. That was fine with me. I was safe indoors, with a cheery little blaze crackling in the fireplace, and dinner steaming on the hearth. The wind and rain blustering around the windows now became a comfortable sound, making the warmth of the fire and the hot dinner in front of me all the more appealing. I draped my blanket over my shoulders, then sat down at the hearth and enjoyed a hearty meal.

About an hour later, still wrapped in the blanket, I lit up my trusty blackthorn pipe and sat back against the mantel-pillar to stretch out my legs and gaze into the fire awhile. I drew gratefully on the pipe, letting the smoke drift from my lips and roil slowly over to the mantelpiece, where the updraft whisked it away up the flue.

But drowsiness was fast overtaking me. It was time to turn in. I did have some qualms about sleeping in this house tonight, mainly because of what dreams might come, but I was so tired and drowsy that sleep was inevitable. I gathered up a few armloads of firewood from the chimney corner and stacked them on the hearth next to my knapsack, then tossed a few pieces on the fire. I glanced at the pocket-watch…about eleven-thirty now. I put the watch on the floor next to the knapsack, making a mental note to wake up somewhere between two and three A.M. to check on the fire. As the fresh wood began to flare and pop on the grate, I crawled into my woolen bedroll and settled my head on the knapsack. In just a few minutes, with the sound of the wind and rain gusting outside, I dropped off to sleep.

2:30 A.M. - I woke up with a jolt; wind whistling, rain still pelting down outside. The fire had burned down a good deal, but it was still throwing out plenty of heat, and the coals glowing at the bottom of the grate bathed the room in a warm, golden light.

I reached out to the stack of wood next to my head. I was just cocking my arm to shot-put one of the locust slabs onto the grate when I noticed a small figure standing in the shadows to one side of the fireplace. It appeared to be a young girl, warming her hands before the fire.

I froze in mid-toss, then, very quietly, I put the log down and tried to make out exactly what I was seeing here. The child huddled by the mantel looked like she had just stepped into the room from some squalid Dickensian orphanage. She was dressed in a filthy lace dressing-gown that dragged on the floor three feet behind her; probably a cast-off from the charity bin of the local madhouse. Under the dressing-gown, she was wrapped in an even filthier, moth-eaten woolen chemise that hung down to her ankles. Her hair was lank, matted, and unkempt; her bare feet were caked in layers of dirt, and the evidence of neglect and malnutrition was shocking to see.

Then the little figure moved into the light, and I noticed that the fire was shining right through her. For a moment, I thought I was gripped in a bad nightmare; but a splinter had gouged into my finger as I placed the log back on the pile, and the pain was quite real. I was not dreaming.

Well...if I still harbored any doubts about who my little visitor was, those doubts were now erased. Here, no more than three feet away, shuffling forward to stand directly in front of me, was the spirit that had animated the face on the wall. As she came closer, an aura of intense cold flowed out before her, enveloping me like a damp burial shroud, and my limbs began to shudder with cold and fear. But the icy embrace that enfolded me didn't feel threatening or evocative of the grave. Instead, I was stricken with a profound sense of sadness, desolation, and loneliness.

The filmy specter halted at the edge of the hearth directly in front of me, inches away, regarding me with a steady gaze. I was gripped with a paralyzing fear, unable to move, barely able to breathe, and my teeth were chattering so loudly I could hear the sound echoing around the empty room. But I knew that now, in spite of fear, I had to sit up and look at this little apparition; look directly into her eyes and listen to her story, no matter how horrifying that story might be. There was no escape. I pushed myself up into a sitting position and wrapped the blanket tighter around me. Then I turned to face the waiting shadow.

As I met the gaze of my ethereal visitor, I was seized by the same galvanizing shock I had felt when I first locked eyes with the image on the wall. But the mood was a little different this time. I was still pierced with waves of sadness and desolation, but underneath those emotions I sensed…curiosity…even friendliness. The icy aura that enfolded me faded away, and I could feel the heat of the fire warming my limbs once again.

My little companion stood motionless before me, less than a foot away, with the wavering firelight shining through her. Her form, which had been shadowy and indistinct, began to grow clear and resolve itself into sharper detail, like a crystalline effigy filled with clear water. I felt the grief and sadness diminish, and I could see the shadow of a smile playing around her lips.

Well…I couldn't help smiling back. I got the feeling this was not an evil spirit, but a lonely and forsaken one; a hungry ghost who needed someone to bear witness to her story. So, once again, in spite of foreboding, I opened my mind to receive whatever the ghost needed to declare. I didn't introduce myself, yet, because I wasn't exactly sure what I was dealing with here. If this apparition in front of me was some kind of demonic spirit or imp, then I would be in mortal danger if it ever learned my name.

"Speak, little one," I said, "let me hear your tale."

The ghost wavered for a moment, a little indecisive now that the moment of catharsis had come upon her. But then she seemed to make up her mind, and sat down in front of me, looking directly into my eyes. A sudden darkness swept through the image, eclipsing the light that had radiated from it moments before. All I could see now was a shadow that looked like outer space, with two cold sparks for eyes.

Again, I invited the ghost to speak. There was a swirling motion like smoke through the shadow, but no other response. I felt the cold aura begin to flow over me again, so I tried another tack: "What's your name, little one?" I asked. There was a moment of hesitation, and the shadow brightened a little. Then I heard a tiny voice echo in my head:

"My name is Abigail, sir. Nabby for short."

I couldn't think of what to say next, so I just blurted out the first thing that popped into my head:

"Abigail…that's a nice name. What's your family name?"

"I'm sorry, sir," said the little voice, "I don't have a family name. I'm sorry."

"Oh, well now…" I stammered out, "you don't have to be sorry, little one. But uhhh…well…I mean…why don't you have a last name, honey?"

Honey? What the hell was I thinking? But I'd never spoken to a ghost before, even in dreams.

"I'm an orphan, sir. My ma and pa left me here at the Sisters of Mercy when I was but five-year-old. The Abbess here, Sister Dagmar, and the other nuns, said my folks didn't want me anymore. And I've been here ever since. I'm sorry to say, sir."

So this place had been a convent and orphanage at one time. That meant my little visitor wasn't a visitor after all. She lived here...so to speak.

But this interview was starting to get painful now. Her parents had dumped her here; just thrown her away, like kicking a bag of garbage off the wagon as they drove by. And then this evil bitch of an abbess and her gang of psychotic nuns tell the little girl her parents didn't want her any more. What kind of vicious rat-bastard says a thing like that to a child, for Chrissakes, even if it *was* true? And how many other and worse outrages had this child suffered? I didn't want to hear any more, and my instincts were screaming at me to get the Hell out of here, right now. But it was too late for that; I was already committed; in for a penny, in for a pound.

"Well...Abigail," I said, "I'm sorry your folks did that to you. That was an evil thing to do. But maybe...maybe you were well rid of a couple of cruel psychopaths like that."

"What kind of paths did you say, sir? I don't know that word." "Sorry, honey," I said, "the word is 'psychopath'. It just means...

well, a bad, mean, evil person."

"Oh," she said, "I see. Yes, sir. They were very mean, bad people.

Both of them. I guess I am well rid of them. But I've been very lonely since then, sir. There's no other children here, and all the Sisters are gone, too. It's just me, now. And my folks took my dear Lilly cat and Bunny Cuddles away...and my Aw-hink and

Cimmie bear too, before they left me here." She was starting to sniffle and weep now.

I wanted to comfort her, somehow, but how do you comfort a ghost? And then this settlement had been abandoned in 1864 and left uninhabited for over one hundred and fifty years, yet my little ghost spoke as if all this had just happened yesterday. Was it possible she didn't realize that she had been dead for a century and a half? That she'd been wandering in an empty village, a *ghost* town, for a very long time?

Well…maybe not. Neither I nor anyone else in this world has the vaguest idea how things work in the spirit realm. Maybe time doesn't work the same there. Or maybe time, as we understand it, doesn't exist there at all. Maybe she thought it was still 1864. Who knew?

One thing for sure, though; it had fallen to me to tell her that she was dead, and a ghost. What happened after that, I had no idea. She was fading in and out now, becoming at times nearly invisible, so I tried to keep the conversation going:

"Uhhh…well, so…how old are you now, honey? How long have you been here at the convent?"

"I'm eight now, sir…I think. And I've been here for about three years now."

Right. Just what I thought. She had no sense of the passage of time. For her, right here and right now, it was the mid-1860's. And my personal attire - the slouch hat, hunting frock and leather leggins of a pre-Revolutionary woodsman - would in no way suggest there was something out of joint in her reckoning. But if she was ever to move on, she would have to be told that it was now the year 2013, and she'd been wandering this place alone for 150 years. "Well…okay…Abigail, so you've been here for three years and you're very lonely, and there's nobody here now. What happened?" She seemed a bit confused at that, but then she answered: "Well, sir, I don't rightly know. I remember I was upstairs looking out the window one day, and all of a sudden there were horse soldiers in butternut...a-runnin' around outside, stealin' everything they could lay their hands on; pigs, cattle, furniture and such, and tossin' it all onto wagons. And they were settin' fire to everything and shootin' the townspeople who were tryin' to get their goods back. I got real scared and hid in the attic."

She was sobbing now, unable to go on. I tossed another log on the fire and waited. Outside, the fury of the storm had grown stronger again; wind screaming with near-hurricane force, rain slapping hard against the roof and walls. It was very unusual for a summer thunderstorm to last this long, and I wondered briefly if this place was catching spin-off storms kicked up by some big hurricane bouncing around in the Gulf of Mexico like a giant pinball. But Abigail had regained her composure, and resumed her narrative:

"Sorry, sir, but I couldn't help thinkin' about my Lilly cat and my Bunny Cuddles. I miss them terribly. They were my only, only, dearest little friends." She wiped away her tears with the edge of her ragged dressing gown, then went on.

"Anyway, things got quiet again after a while, so I came back down to the main room here, and..."

She stopped in mid-sentence, hesitating to go on. That didn't bode well, but I figured she needed to get it all out, no matter how bad it was.

"So what did you see, honey? Did the soldiers break in here? What happened?"

She sobbed convulsively a few more times, then continued her narration. But she was clearly afraid to go on; afraid to stir up even the memory of it.

"Well…I got down to the bottom of the stairs…and then I heard…something…I didn't know what…so I opened the door just a crack, and peeked out…and then, there was…screaming… all this terrible…*terrible…screaming.*"

The shadow in front of me suddenly went black, and her voice choked with terror and grief. I felt the grave-cold aura reaching out to envelop me again. A few more moments passed in silence, so I encouraged her to say on:

"What happened, Nabby? Who was screaming? What did you see?"

"It was the nuns that were screaming. The soldiers…the soldiers…had broke in…and they drove all the nuns into the main room, right here, with big knives on the ends of their muskets, and made them get down on their knees."

"Those are called bayonets, Abigail." I added. So they used fixed bayonets to herd the nuns into the main room; carefully out of sight of the townsfolk. This didn't sound like it was going to end well.

"Bayonets…yes! I remember now…that's what they called them. And then…and then…this big, tall man with a black moustache and a black hat, smoking a seegar, stepped through the door and stomped around the room in his big, black boots. And he was a-grinnin', too, with his big, ugly yellow teeth. And he said, in a real loud voice, loudest voice I ever did hear, that everybody in this village was a traitor to the Southern Confederacy, especially these damned nuns…and that he, Colonel Clay Allison, second in command to General Forrest and his cavalry, was gonna damn well see to it that this town and everybody in it was punished for their treason…startin' with these damned nuns." Here she paused again, sobbing uncontrollably.

'Colonel' Clay Allison, eh? I knew that name.

Clay Allison was one of the most cruel, sadistic, psychotic outlaws in the post-Civil War West. He was with Nathan Bedford Forrest's Confederate Raiders during the war, but was drummed out by Forrest, personally, for excessive violence and insanity. After the war, he went on to become a charter member of the Ku Klux Klan, and in 1887 died in a richly ironic freak accident when his neck was crushed under the wheels of a manure wagon.

So poor little Abigail had been an unwilling witness to one of Clay Allison's many bloodbaths, in this case while he was with a rogue element of the Confederate cavalry. There was absolutely no question, now, that I didn't want to hear any more of this story.

But this wasn't about me anymore. This little waif had undoubtedly witnessed a mind-blasting atrocity, perpetrated by one of the most cruel, insane, and bloodthirsty murderers ever to walk the earth. And if she was ever to quit her lonely haunting of this place and enter into the light, she needed to tell the story, purge herself of the horror, and escape her dismal fate.

"So what happened then, Abigail? Can you remember?"
"Well…he had Sister Dagmar dragged in, and they threw her down on her knees in front of the Colonel. And she was beggin' for her life and for the other nuns. He listened for a while, a-grinnin' and a-laughin'. But then…then…he tore off her wimple, grabbed her by the back of her neck, and…God help me…he twisted the burning end of his seegar into her eyes! And Sister Dagmar screamed like a hog bein' slaughtered, and all the other nuns were screamin', too. He yelled at her to shut the Hell up, but she couldn't stop screamin', so he kicked her over on her

back…and she still didn't stop screamin'…so he grabbed a musket from one of the soldiers, and he…he…stepped on her neck with his big, black boot, then drove the bayonet into her eye…so hard that it went right through her head and pinned her to the floor! And then he and the other soldiers hooted and laughed and clapped their hands, and some of 'em danced a little jig while Sister Dagmar was twitchin' and kickin' and bleedin' on the floor! Oh God…it was terrible! I can't stand thinkin' about it! I wish I'd never seen it!" She broke down and wailed, shrinking into a little black shadow on the floor now.

Jesus Christ! I thought…this was worse than anything I could have imagined. And I knew we weren't done yet…not if Allison lived up to his reputation for studied brutality.

Outside, the storm raged on unabated. I glanced at my pocket watch…3:30 AM. Only an hour had gone by, but I was soaked with sweat and shuddering as if I had been on a torture rack for days. I hardly dared to ask what happened next, but we had to keep moving.

"I'm sorry you had to see that, Abigail. Clay Allison was a cruel man, one of the cruelest who ever lived. But it might ease your mind a little to know that he didn't escape retribution for his evil deeds. His neck was crushed under a wagon a few years later in a gruesome accident, and he's been roasting in Hell ever since. I hope that helps."

The little shadow on the floor brightened up a bit, looking more like a child again. But then suspicion crept into her voice:

"You knew Colonel Allison, sir? How could you know him? Were you one of his troopers?"

"No, honey. I never knew Allison. But I've read something about him…in history books."

"In history books? But this only happened a year ago. How could he be in history books already? What…?"

"I'll explain later, honey," I interrupted, "when you're finished with your story. I'm going to have to get moving come sunrise…if it's not still raining, and that's only a few hours away now."

She started to wail again. "Oh no! Please don't go! Don't leave me! I've been so lonely for so long now…and you're the first person I've spoken to in a year! Oh, please don't go…please!" She was weeping now, but she managed to stammer out between sobs: "Or maybe…maybe you could take me with you? I don't have anybody here. My Lilly cat and Bunny Cuddles are gone, and they were my only friends. I'd just as soon go with you now."

Well…what the hell was I gonna do with that? I couldn't stay here, even if I wanted to. I needed to get moving, soon, for a great many reasons; but mainly because just being here inside this house was almost certainly illegal. And I sure couldn't take Abigail with me. She was a ghost.

I let out a long sigh. "I'll explain it all when you're finished telling your story, Abigail. I really can't stay here, and I really can't take you with me, much though I might like that. You'll understand perfectly when I explain it to you. And it might not be as bad as you think. Meantime, why don't you tell me the rest of it?"

"I don't want to now," she said, voice thick with weeping, "if you're gonna leave me here all alone. And…I don't even know your name, sir."

"Well…I can at least fix that, Abigail, honey. My name is John Henry Ferguson, and I'm very pleased to know you."

"John Henry?" she said, brightening. "I like that." And then she started sniffling again. "But I can't talk about it. I can't bear to remember it. It was terrible."

"I'm sure it was, Nabby…I'm sure it was. And I don't really want to hear any more of it either. But you need to get all this off your chest, honey. You won't be able to escape this wretched place until you do."

After a long silence, she said, very quietly, "Escape this place? Whatever do you mean, John Henry…escape this place?"

Oops. Cat's out of the bag now. Well…it had to be done. Just as well to tell her now as later.

"Well…Nabby honey…I don't know exactly how to say this…so I'm just gonna say it. Do you know what year it is now?"

"That's a strange question, sir. I can't understand why you'd ask it. But if you must know, why, it's 1865, of course. I remember reading it in a newspaper one of the soldiers left on the fireplace when they skedaddled out of here…on July 5th, 1864, right after the battle over to Gettysburg. So it would be 1865 now. But why do you ask such a silly question?"

"Well, Nabby…I'm afraid that's not exactly true. You see, actually, it's now July 5th, 2013…one hundred and fifty years later. I'm sorry…there's just no other way to say it."

There was a shocked silence from the little ghost. Then, in a tiny voice, she whispered: "What…?"

"It's the year of our Lord 2013 now, Nabby," I said. I pulled out the tourist brochure I had found earlier, showing her the cover page with the date. "Here…take a look," I said, holding the pamphlet up to the light. For a long moment, she just stared at it, saying nothing. Then she reached out to grab the pamphlet for a closer look, and her ghostly hand passed right through it. She tried again, and again her insubstantial hand passed through it like fog. Badly shaken now, she stared at her hand, then turned and looked at me, eyes wide with fear.

"John Henry…why can't I lay my hands on that thing? They're just…it's like they're not there. What's happening? Am I dreaming…or losing my mind? Oh…what's happening, John Henry? I'm scared!"

"Well, Nabby, I'm sorry to have to tell you this…and again, there's no good way to put it…the reason you can't touch this pamphlet, honey, is because you're a ghost…a spirit. It's not 1864 now…it's 2013, a hundred and fifty years later, yet you're still a child, Nabby, you haven't aged at all. So you must have…crossed over…sometime shortly after the soldiers were here. Do you remember anything about that, Nabby? About…well…your last day of life?"

A great silence fell over us. The storm continued to howl outside, but there was absolute stillness within. Then a shrill, animal keening, horrible to hear, issued from the little spirit.

"I don't believe it, John Henry," she wailed, "it can't be true…it just can't be true! I can't be **dead**! I can't be a ghost!"

The anguish that now tormented the poor little spirit wrung my heart with fear and pity. But it was more important than ever now that she remember the whole story, especially the part leading up to her death, which almost certainly happened while Allison was at the climax of his butcheries. I waited a few moments for her to calm down, then I urged her to finish her narrative:

"Nabby…please…listen to me. You've got to remember everything that happened that day. You've got to finish your story, honey. Because I think when you get to the end of it, you're gonna remember how you…passed into the spirit world. I know it was terrible, but it's over…it's been over for a long, long time now…a hundred and fifty years. And once you realize that, you'll finally be free, and you can stop haunting this place and go to the light… maybe see your little friends again. That doesn't sound too bad, does it?"

"I don't know, John Henry," she sobbed. "I don't know what to think." Then she started wailing again: "Oh, dear God!...what's to become of me!? What's to become of me!? I'm scared, John Henry! And I've been all alone here since that terrible...terrible day when..." She stopped, choked with grief and horror, unable to go on.

"Tell me Nabby," I said quietly. "Tell me all of it. And don't worry what's going to become of you. There is nothing in Heaven or Earth that can harm you now. You're beyond all that...all of it. What's ahead for you, from now on, is only good. *That* I can promise you."

I checked my pocket watch again. 5:00 A.M. now – not much longer 'til daybreak.

"Now, please Nabby...get it off your chest. We've only got a few more hours. What happened next?"

"Well...he wasn't done yet, the rotten bastard. After Sister Dagmar stopped kicking and screaming, she...she died. He must have enjoyed that, because he ordered his men to strip the rest of the nuns naked, all ten of them, and then pin them to the floor with bayonets, arms and legs, like Jesus on the cross. Then they... the soldiers...well, I don't rightly know what it was they did...but the Colonel called them in from outside, and they all lined up and, one by one, pulled their pants down and got on top of the nuns and...it must have been something bad, what they did, because the nuns were all screamin' and begging for mercy." She paused for a moment, weeping inconsolably, but she regained control of herself, and then continued:

"It was terrible...all that screaming...and blood all soaking into the carpet and all over the floor...blood everywhere. I couldn't watch anymore, so I climbed up the stairs and clapped my hands over my ears."

"But I could still hear them screaming…for a long time…even after the soldiers left, galloping away on their horses. After a while, I came back down and pushed the door all the way open." Then her voice cracked with horror as she recounted the grisly scene that lay before her:

"Oh God, John Henry…I hope never, never to see a thing like that again. The nuns…they were all dead…just layin' there on the floor. And the floor…and the carpets…were all soaked with blood…swimming in blood…in a big pool…right up to the stairway. I didn't dare to step off the stairs onto the floor…it was all so bloody. But that wasn't the worst of it. They had…the soldiers… had slit the Sisters bellies open and pulled out their insides, like hogs. And left their bayonets stickin' up in 'em. And there was a terrible stink, like a slaughterhouse! God…it was…I can't stand to think of it anymore!"

I wanted to pat her on the shoulder, or embrace her…comfort her somehow; try to assuage her terrifying memories. But of course, there was nothing I could do. Not in the face of that kind cruelty and slaughter.

"I'm so sorry, dear little Nabby," I whispered. "There's no consolation for having to witness a bloody slaughter like that. I can only offer the hope of Heaven for you as recompense."

"Thank you, John Henry…that does help...but it wasn't over yet. I was just looking over the blood and dead bodies, and shakin' and cryin'…and all of a sudden, that God damned Colonel Allison stepped around a corner, I don't know from where, and he had blood drippin' from his jowls, like some kind of…blood-drinking… *monster*."

"Then he saw me standing there, looking at him. I turned and ran back up the stairway, and he came runnin' after me…I could hear his boots a-thumpin' across the floor. I just about got to the top of the stair when there was great big BOOM, and a sledgehammer hit me in the back. Then I fell down. But I got back up again and ran and hid behind the upstairs chimney. But the floor back there was rotten, and I fell down between the chimney and the wall. And I got stuck there…I couldn't get loose. I heard his boots a-stumpin' around for a while…then I heard a horse galloping away. After that, everything got quiet."

"I tried hard to get loose, but I couldn't get unstuck, no matter what. I tried yelling, but nobody answered. Then, after a while, I got tired and sleepy, and the place where the bullet hit me was hurting real bad, and my back was all wet, and then…I guess…I just… fell asleep." She hesitated, as if some new thought had suddenly occurred to her. The truth was beginning to dawn on her now.

"When did you wake up Nabby?" I said, "what's the next thing you remember?"

"Well…the next thing I remember is…I woke up next to the fireplace down here. I don't know how I got there. And I was all alone. And I wasn't in pain anymore. All the bodies were gone…and the whole place was empty…no carpets, no blood, no chandelier, no pictures, no nuns…nothing. I went to the front door…it was open…and looked outside. It was snowing pretty hard, but I didn't feel the least bit cold, so I went down the steps and into the village to see if I could find somebody who could tell me what happened. But I couldn't find anybody, not a living soul…anywhere. All the people were gone." She stopped for a moment, still mystified by what she had found in the village.

"The whole town was deserted then?"

"Yes, John Henry…they were all gone. I walked around the whole settlement, one end to the other, calling out for somebody to help me. But nobody came. Most of the houses were gone, too.

Some of them had burnt down, but most of them were just caved in, covered with weeds and vines, like they'd tumbled down a long time ago. The whole place was deserted, like you said."

"So, what did you do then?"

"Well…I couldn't find anybody, and the snow was getting deeper, and I was feeling terribly lonely, and there were horrible *things* creeping around through the snowflakes, and the wind was shrieking up in the trees, so I ran back here to the convent. I went out a few more times, in case any of the people came back. But they never did, so after a while, I just didn't go out anymore."

"You never went out again?"

"No…never."

"So…how did you feed yourself? How did you stay warm? How did you occupy your time?"

She was a little nonplussed by the question, but then, after some thought, she came up with a tentative explanation:

"Well, John Henry…I guess I just never felt hungry…or cold. And for a while, I just wandered around the house. But I got so very lonely as the days went by. So…I curled up next to the mantel here and went to sleep. And when I woke up, you were here, and there was a fire in the fireplace, and the door was shut, and I thought maybe I wasn't going to be lonely anymore." Then she broke down sobbing again.

"But now you say you're going to leave when the sun comes up…you're going to leave me here, and I'll be all alone again. I'm scared of this place! There are monsters here, terrible ghosts, and I don't want to stay here anymore! I want to go with you, John Henry! Why can't you take me with you? I thought you were my friend! Oh, why can't you take me with you? Why?"

This was getting unbearable now. I would have taken her with me in a heartbeat, if that were possible. She certainly deserved better than what she had gotten in life. But she had departed this life…she was a ghost, doomed to walk this place alone forever, and there was nothing I could do for her.

But wait…maybe there *was* something I could do for her. She said she had fallen down into the space between the wall and the chimney and got stuck, and died there with Clay Allison's bullet in her back. That meant that her body, or what was left of it, was probably still lodged there, right behind that stain on the wall. So maybe…just maybe, if I could free her body from the wall and give it a proper burial, then her spirit would be released from its fate, and she could go to God.

This I *would* do. But first, I needed to prepare her for what I was intending to do, which might get very ugly in a hurry.

"Nabby, honey, I would take you with me if I could. But I can't, because you're a ghost. You were shot in the back by Clay Allison, fell down between the wall and the chimney, got wedged there, and…I'm sorry to put it so bluntly…you bled out and died there. That was 1864, Nabby. It's July, 2013 now. You've been wandering alone in this place, as a ghost, for one hundred and fifty years. Did you ever wonder why you never felt cold, or hungry, or why you can't touch anything? It's because you're not in your body anymore, Nabby; you're in the spirit world now. And, for some reason I don't understand, you're trapped here in this dreadful place; doomed to walk alone…your immortal soul trapped between Heaven and Hell, until something changes."

She was very quiet now, shrunk down to a small shadow on the hearth. I could barely hear her breathing. Then she said:

"John Henry…I'm so afraid of this place…I'm so lonely…I miss my little friends…I even miss the nuns…and I don't want to be here anymore. You're my best and only friend. Can't you help me…somehow?"

"Yes, Nabby...I think I can help you...to escape your doom, anyway. But in order to do that, I'm going to have to do something really nasty. I'm going to have to disinter your body from that wall over there, and give you a decent burial...out in the forest, away from this accursed place. Once that's been done, I think you'll be free to leave here...go to God...maybe even see your little friends again. How would that be?"

"Well...if you think that will break the curse that's on me, then... go ahead and do it. Free my soul, John Henry. Let me go to God."

"You realize you're a ghost then, Nabby?"

"Yes, John Henry...I can't deny it anymore. I took a bullet in my back...I remember it now. I couldn't live after that. Nobody could." "No, Nabby...you took a mortal wound from that murdering swine," I said. "But remember...all the pain and terror are over. Nothing can harm you now. You only have Heaven to look forward to."

I pulled my tomahawk, then walked over to the mantelpiece and started chopping out a large circle in the wall around the stain where I guessed her remains were still lodged. Big chunks of plaster came tumbling down from the wall, clattering and thudding to the floor, kicking up a thick cloud of dust as I hacked away. Finally, after about a half-hour's work, I levered the last few gritty lumps of plaster away from the ancient lathing and stood back to see what I had uncovered.

At first, all I could see was a huge cloud of dust billowing up in front of the fireplace, and damned little else. It was still dark and raining outside, and the fire had burned down to coals while I had been engaged with Nabby's ghost, so I tossed a few logs on the fire and waited. After a few minutes, the fresh wood flared up and threw off enough light for me to get a better look at the exposed section of the wall. The space between the chimney and the wall lathing was only about six inches wide, and narrowed to nothing as the chimney descended to, and then joined the fireplace. So once Nabby got wedged in there, she was too weak to claw her way out, especially with a large caliber lead ball buried in her spine.

There was a nasty, dark stain in the lathing where she had bled out and then melted into the slats as her body decayed. The wood around the little corpse had almost completely rotted away over the next century and a half, so I had no trouble chopping that segment out of the surrounding slats. As it came loose from the wall, I took care to lower the piece down to the floor slowly and respectfully, since I was basically removing a dead body from its resting place.

The light from the fire had grown stronger with the fresh wood I had thrown on, and it illuminated the poor thing lying on the hearth with pitiless clarity. There wasn't much left of her after a century and a half – a small, desiccated skeleton fused to the wooden slats, with a few rags of dried skin still hanging from the ribs; arms and legs sagged down as she bled out and went limp with death. And most pitiful of all…her face was turned upwards towards the light in a final gesture of despair and sorrow.

I knelt down to study how best to separate the remains from the rotten lathing, and caught sight of the lead ball lodged in her spine just next to the left shoulder blade. It was amazing that she was able to get up and run after a heavy slug like that slammed into her. And the shot was cruelly placed, too, meant to maim, but not kill; probably delivered from a LeMat cavalry revolver; a massive, .42 caliber pistol capable of knocking a horse out from under a rider with one shot.

And Allison had used that brutal weapon to murder a little girl. I felt my heart filling up with hate as I thought of that subhuman maggot deliberately killing Nabby; for no reason at all, other than to indulge his own filthy, sadistic pleasure. I covered my face and wept with rage and pity. Then I felt the little ghost move next to me, and she spoke words of comfort:

"Please don't cry, John Henry," she whispered, "it doesn't hurt anymore. And like you said, all of that happened a hundred and fifty years ago. And…I think I'm ready to go now…now that I know you'll take care of my poor body. They're waiting for me up there…I hear their gentle voices calling. Please don't cry. I can't bear your tears, John Henry."

She was right, of course. I got a grip on myself and stood up, mopping my eyes with my neckerchief. Then I looked up and noticed that the rain had stopped, and it was beginning to get light outside. I stepped over to the window to get a better view. It was still pretty dark out yet, but the heavy clouds were hurrying along close overhead now; the sun breaking through in places, sending shafts of light slanting down from the clouds. Then the room suddenly lit up behind me.

I turned and saw Nabby, no longer a diminutive little shadow in the corner, but standing in the middle of the room, radiating light like the morning Sun through church windows. She stepped towards me, smiling like an angel.

"Oh, look, John Henry," she said, laughing in an outburst of pure joy, pointing to the stairway door, "they've come to take me home…my dear little Lilly cat, and Bunny Cuddles! Oh…look! There they are, right in front of me! Oh my God…oh my God! I'm so glad to see you again my dear little friends! You came back… you came back at last! Are you here to take me to Heaven my dear little friends? Yes! Yes! Oh yes!…I will come with you!" Then she turned to me.

"Oh…I'm sorry, John Henry, my best and only friend, I'm so sorry! But I can go home now…I don't have to stay here in this terrible house anymore! But I'll always remember you…my dear friend who helped me to escape this place forever. Please bury my body, away from here; out there under the big apple tree in the woods, up on a hill…you'll know the one when you see it."

"I promise, little Nabby. I'll bury you under that apple tree. Go now, dear little Nabby, and Godspeed."

She moved toward the stairway door, light blazing from her like a meteor. As she reached the door, she turned and raised her hand in a final farewell. "Goodbye, John Henry," she said, "I will pray for you." Then she was gone.

"Goodbye, dear Nabby," I whispered, "Go to God."

Up in the sky, the clouds parted for a moment, and a bright shaft of sunlight streamed down into the room, there to catch the soul. Then the flickering beam moved on across the open fields and faded from view.

I just stood there by the window for a while, the sun glaring in hot through the glass as it rose into the morning sky. But I couldn't stand there for long; I had promised Nabby to bury her body before I left, and I needed to get the job done before it got too hot out. I pulled my 'hawk' and chopped most of the rotten lathing slats away from the body, then wrapped it up in my blanket roll. I packed up the rest of my kit, slung my rifle, and took a final look around. The fire had long since burned out, but I banked it anyway, just to be sure the village didn't disappear in a roaring firestorm after I left. Then, cradling Nabby's remains under one arm, I headed for the cellar stairway. A few moments later, I climbed up the granite stairs from the basement and shut the hatch behind me. Then I turned and leaned on my rifle, studying the woods behind the house, wondering if I could ever find the apple tree Nabby mentioned. Her memory of it dated from 1864, and the thing might have fallen over and rotted away a long time ago.

But after about an hour of clambering through the wet, tangled blow-down, I found the venerable old tree standing by itself on a wind-swept knoll that rose a good twenty feet above the rest of the forest. It was huge and ancient - its knobby trunk at least four feet thick, topped with a great crown of gnarled branches that reached fifty feet into the sky, swathed with silver-green leaves that fluttered and sparkled in the wind - a worthy final resting place for anyone.

I climbed the embankment and walked slowly around the tree's great bole, looking for likely places to lay Nabby's bones to rest. Luckily, I found a cranny on the west side of the tree that opened into its hollowed-out heart. I unwrapped the body and lowered it down into the crevice until I felt it hit bottom. Over the top of the cranny, I carved the epitaph: "Abigail – Orphan and Child Of God Died July 4, 1864" Finally, I sprinkled a few pinches of tobacco around the tree and closed the ceremony with the words: "May God welcome your spirit into Heaven, and wipe away your tears forever, dear Nabby. I'm sorry I couldn't do more for you. Ho… Mitakuye Oyasin."

I raised my hand in a final farewell, then cinched up my knapsack, slung my rifle, and headed for the path out of the settlement. In all the days since then, I've kept little Nabby in my prayers, and ask her to watch over me from the spirit world as I walk through this life.

By my hand this day - July 5, 2013 - *John Henry Ferguson* – The Median Man

The End

CASE #52071

THE JOURNAL OF THE MEDIAN MAN - A FACE ON THE WALL

BY BARRY PRICE

Barry Price was born in Baltimore, Maryland into a long line of story-tellers. After graduating from Towson University in 1978, Barry spent two years of study at the Actor's Conservatory in Baltimore, where he made his stage debut in 1983. He turned professional in 1986, appearing in many stage productions in Baltimore and Washington, D.C. - most notably in Richard III at the Shakespeare Theatre at the Folger Library, directed by Michael Kahn, with Stacey Keach in the title role.

In 1995, Barry won a principal role in the 1996 cult hit sci-fi movie, Twelve Monkeys. As Secret Service Agent #1, he worked closely with Brad Pitt, Bruce Willis, and Director Terry Gilliam in a number of dramatic and stunt scenes, utilizing his abilities as an actor and a black-belt stunt performer.

Barry retired from professional show-business in 2001 to pursue a career in writing, and in 2003 wrote "Day Player – Tales from the Dark Side of Acting in the Movies", a humorous memoir of his adventures in the movie business. "The Journal of the Median Man – A Face on the Wall", is his first short story in the Median Man series.

The Cottonwood Curse by John Beechem

I WRITE THESE WORDS AS A MAN determined to die. My life is one of pain, despair, addiction and grief. To extinguish the spark of my life would be to smother a doomed flame, a flickering wick of grief trapped inside a human being. Its cessation would be a mercy. Not only to me, but to those whose lives are intertwined with the thread of my own.

The doctors tell me I am a mortal case, and I believe them. Three years ago, a sojourn to a drier clime would bring me relief, if sometimes a stinging sunburn. Now it brings me nothing but frightened stares and bloody handkerchiefs. Consumption. The bloody lunged blighter grants her scarlet kiss to the just and the unjust alike, but I am more deserving of her greedy lips than any other, I'd wager.

In the grandstand, they situate themselves far from me now. I tire of staining countless linen scraps; now I simply tie a piece of silk around my face, laced with a touch of *parfum* to ward off the smell of manure. My family helped fund the construction of Churchill Downs, so even with my affliction, none dare turn me away.

Howard accompanies me. He oft reminisces about his boyhood labors in my father's stable, tells me which colt to place a bet on when my mind is too scattered to decide, and is quick to fetch bourbon and tobacco when the need arises. I allow him to take off his servant's coat on days that it is warm, and we roll up the sleeves of our shirts, and watch the races together. Although he is a son of Ham, Howard has a keen mind, and a serpent's tongue. He tells me God has damned me for the deeds I've done, and my crimes are so wicked, my life has become a hell on earth. "Just a warm breath compared to what waits for you, Mr. Bingham," he often taunts. I am inclined to agree. Howard Freeman is a bastard in every sense of the word, but I've grown fond of him. He's clever as far as bastards go, and in exchange for his care unto my death, I have written him the sum of $7,000 to be bequeathed from my will, one that will provide well for his wife and their brood, which now numbers nine if my memory serves. Indeed, it is my cursed memory that torments me.

The evil night that plagues my mind was almost half a decade ago. It was in the final days of the Southern Exposition, illuminated by crackling electric lanterns swarmed by moths, a Saturday evening among the dozens of new mansions built in the past few years. Mine stands tall in Belgravia Court, close to 4th Street for the convenience of our late cantankerous carriage driver, Howard's father Philip. God rest his soul, he is among the departed.

I digress. Please pardon the chaos of these scribbles; their meanderings are evidence of a scattered mind. Lilian was with me that night, my golden haired wife, at the height of her beauty in her twenty-first year. I was entering my twenty-six. She was of Sanders stock, so her father and half her uncles were Kentucky Colonels. My father suggested our courtship, hungry for a large dowry, I've no doubt. He holds me in contempt, the miserable old man, and knows the depths of my vices make me ill-suited for industrious work. My best hope, he always told me, was to charm a poor, little rich girl, one lonely and with a heart aching for loss. I followed his advice, and caught the eye of the young widow, Lilian Sanders, at a Wednesday night picnic, the spring before my consumption became evident.

In half a dozen months, we wed, and in a display of wealth worthy of Midas, Lilian's father paid for the construction of our home as part of her dowry. I also received a quarter of the home's value in cash, in part to pay for our furnishings. I put the remainder into an account, a little nest egg for the both of us, for when we would start producing heirs of our own.

This would provide for education at the university, finery to distinguish their level of birth, and other trappings of wealth in this so-called Gilded Age.

Excess was evident that night at the Exposition. We were newly-weds out for a night time stroll. Our ears were piqued by the sound of a guitar, one plucked by skilled and nimble hands. A young black man in a bright blue suit, his eyes twinkling with the mischief of a dandy, was playing "Oberon". It was a song he played often and well. My wife stopped, and we turned to listen. His gaze caught Lilian's eye and he bowed his head. The tune changed abrupty, and he strummed a song with lyrics sprung from cupid's heart. He had a mythical talent, to be sure, but all the pluck of the gods as well, to make such a bold display before my own wife.

In a flash of hot anger, I pulled Lilian away from him. I decided it was high time to walk down Park Avenue to meet my bookie, Charles Dorsey. He owed me money for a wager I'd made on a ball game between Louisville and Cincinnati; the local boys lost (as I knew we would–I had made specific arrangements) and I was about to collect a tidy sum. My gambling habit upset Lilian, but it made her secret love of the poppy less damning, so in a tenuous truce, we agreed to discuss neither.

Of course, she began to protest as we left the guitar player far behind.

"Damn you, Robert! That boy was splendid. Why don't you ever want to stop and listen to the world for a moment?" Her anger was palpable, if a bit silly.

I sighed, and pulled my watch from my vest pocket. I flipped its gold lid, checked the time, and explained, "Dorsey said 9:00 P.M. It's a quarter to the hour, and I find it prudent to collect on my wager before his other clients come calling. Forget the darkie; I'll have Howard to play his banjo for us tonight."

***

At the stroke of three, I woke, and found my bed empty. Lilian and I slept together every night. After I satisfied my masculine desires with an empathic rapidity, I would roll onto my back and sleep. If I woke to fill the chamber pot, Lillian would be asleep, curled away from me. Tonight, she was absent.

I pulled on my robe , and grabbed a pistol from the bureau. *Where had she gone?*

I found them in the billiard room. The cries of their beastly coitus could be heard from the library. The room had a lock, but as master of the house, I carry a skeleton key with me at all times. In case a member of weaker sex is to find and recover this journal, I will spare your fragile heart the details, but let it be said, their debauchery would have made Bacchus and Venus proud.

The pair stopped; their eyes turned toward me. The young musician turned from my wife and faced me, pulling his blue breeches back on and tying his belt. His arousal made this a difficult task, to say the least.

My wife made no attempt at modesty, and laughed cruelly. "Guitar ain't the only thing he's good at. Is that pistol even loaded?"

I remember nothing but my vision flooding red. In a moment, my ears deafened by the crack of the shot, I opened my eyes, and saw Lilian's blood and brains spread upon the pool table. I looked at the smoking gun in my hand, and felt a moment of dread. Then, the dark machinations of my mind began to turn, and I thought of a scheme.

I struck the guitar player's face with the butt of my pistol. Abraham Greene; I would learn his name when I read the newspaper the next morning. The boy fell to the floor, and I picked him up by his ruffled collar. "You're coming with me, Orpheus."

With the barrel of the pistol in his back, I directed Abraham to the door. I kicked him down the steps, and called to the bemused crowd gathering on the walkway in front of my home. They were strolling past, revelers who'd left the Exposition and had been on their way home. "This man slew my wife!" I roared. "He came into my home, raped my darling Lilian, and with his lustful thirst slaked, put a bullet into her head. What say ye, gentlemen, ye sons of the Confederacy?" A few turned away, shaking their heads, and cursing. Half a dozen others looked up at Abraham, their liquored eyes glazed with bloodlust.

A member of the local constabulary, soaked to the gills but with a yeoman's constitution, came up to us both. "This one's not fit for the courtroom. We'll take our vengeance now."

We formed a mob, and marched north to Floral Terrace. To the lynching tree. Someone grabbed a rope, and then the dandy's face was wrought in a coward's acceptance of death. He stared at me with pleading eyes, his face wet with tears and blood. In minutes, we reached the tree, a tall cottonwood. I grinned, poking him in the chest with the pistol's barrel as the rope was tightened around his neck. The constable threw it over one of the limbs, and a trio of brawny men pulled Abraham high into the air.

His death did not take long. When it was over, when I was certain, I fired a pair of shots into the air, and returned home. I told Howard to allow the magistrates to enter the estate, and arrange to have Lilian's body taken away. I made arrangements to contact her father.

***

After Lilian's death, I spent much of her father's fortune in the brothels. I was intelligent enough to protect myself against Nature's punishment for fornication, but tuberculosis came to me instead. In the remaining years of my life, I vowed, I would have a lifetime's worth of experiences. I traveled down the Mississippi in an opulent steam-ship, sailed near Cuba and the Bahamas, drank a crate's worth of absinthe, smoked hashish by the pound, and gambled my life's fortune away. It did nothing but numb the pain which would inevitably return.

And so I waited for my life to end.

Three days ago, I began to hear the tune of Oberon in my ears wherever I would go. I'd shut my bedroom's window, but the sound would not diminish. Even with the bellowing of a trumpet in my parlor or the roar of an elephant, most likely, nothing could push the dreaded melody from my mind.

But this night, I have found it. I have traced its source, in the light of the full moon, to that tree in Floral Terrace. I walked the blocks north in my bed-robe, my pistol to protect me from scoundrels, and my journal to record my observations. As soon as I viewed the blonde leaved-tree, the sounds of Oberon ceased as if a conductor had willed it.

I stared up into the branches of the tall cottonwood. Somewhere an owl hooted, and a bat flew from its arboreal perch, into a cloud of insects basking in Luna's glow. I saw Abraham, hanging. I see him now. No longer corporeal, his spirit glows a dim blue. Abraham's clothes are tattered, but his face is no longer tear-streaked. He looks down at me. He is waiting.

In front of the trunk, someone has placed a pile of black lilies.

For me, I realize.

Tomorrow is the day of all Souls. I will see Lilian in Hell, but I never want to see Abraham again.

The End.

CASE #84071

THE COTTONWOOD CURSE
BY JOHN BEECHEM

John Beechem is a writer from Louisville, Kentucky. He self-publishes on his website American Fantastic (<u>americanfantastic.com</u>), a community for writers and artists of all kinds. John has been published locally in the Cavalcade Literary Magazine and Tobacco Magazine. He hosts the American Fantastic Radio Hour on ARTxFM (<u>artxfm.com</u>), a community radio station, and has also hosted Keep Louisville Literary, also on ARTxFM.

His writing encompasses many pulp genres, including horror, fantasy, and science fiction. John also writes some poetry and literary fiction. He hopes to entertain his audience, to help them escape the reality of their day to day world, but also to inject higher themes and complex characters into his stories to create quality middle-brow writing. John is influenced by writers like George R.R. Martin, Margaret Atwood, and Octavia Butler, but also by video games, comic books, and other elements of pop culture.

If you would like to learn more about John or his website American Fantastic, you can follow American Fantastic on Facebook or e-mail John at americanfantastic@gmail.com .
John lives with his wife, Kelly. He looks forward to the grand adventure that life has to offer them.

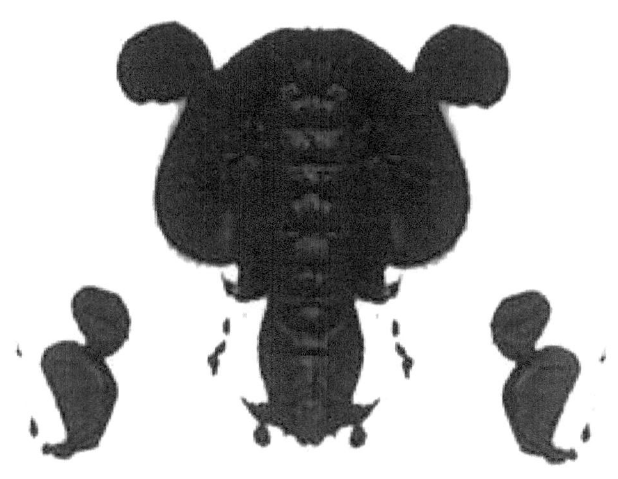

Jesus Fuck: or The Beheading by Jay Helmstutler

I.

You stare at your face long enough in a mirror at night and
you can scare yourself. You stare one long time into the face
of darkness and you can end up fucked for life.

Nine nights ago, the face of darkness appeared on my
computer screen and I stared right into it. I watched through
my fingers as a man had his head sawed off by a group of
masked executioners. I listened as his screams filled the room
until there was only the silent image of his severed head being
lifted by its hair.

And oh God the dead silence when they finally dangled his
head before the camera. I have never heard silence like that—a
deathly hum of audible silence that spread throughout the
room and then the entire house—a silence that has since been
replaced by strange clicks and taps in the middle of the night.

II.

The middle of the night.
There aren't any words for the middle of the night. Words
have no power then—not when you're trying to make your
way through the darkened house and your mind is playing
games with you. The only word that really comes to mind is
Jesus. Jesus and *fuck*. Sometimes you say *fuck, Jesus* and
sometimes *Jesus, fuck*. Sometimes the words just run through
your mind and you can't get them out, and it wouldn't even
help if you could. The only noises in the house are these odd
little clicks and taps and you think to yourself, *everything
should be quiet if I'm the only one moving; if I'm the only living
presence in the house*. But then there's another little click or tap
and that's when *Jesus, fuck* comes out of your mouth or at

least rings as loud in your mind as the sound of those
  godawful screams in that clip you just
had to go and dare yourself to watch.

III.
The terrible commotion of the noise in that
clip *Allahu Akbar* they shout
Their shouts mingling with his horrible
screams Aaaaahhhhh
His screams rising
Aaaaaaahhhhhhhhhhhhhhhhhh
Aaaallaaaahhh
Aahhhhhhh
The gurgled screams are his
God's
My own
Everyone's
We're all going to die this way
By the hands of a devil with a knife
And terror will reign when freedom no longer
rings Amen

IV.
There has to be some light in these words to counteract what I
have seen. I have to find some order in this—or at least a way to
walk through my own house at night without being afraid. For a
darkness has a hold on me, a darkness outside of me or inside of
me, I'm not sure which. But I am captive to its power ever since
watching that clip.

Make me un-watch it, make me never have to watch it again—
in my head or anywhere else. Let the images not come tonight, let
them never come again. Let the sun come up now and let it stay,

let the night never return: the night I used to cherish, that I now
fear. My imagination, that used to be my escape, that I am
now trying to escape *from*: unrecognizably blackened, charred,
so that there are no more light images, no more brightness, just
bleakness, blackness, not even dusk, only nightfall, and I am
falling, befallen by this sensation I can't shake. Shake me, wake
me from this nightmare marring the night; leave me not alone
in this place with my imagination, for I am afraid that it will
destroy me.

V.

Don't ever watch that clip.

Yet if someone had told me that nine nights ago, I
wouldn't have believed them and would have still indulged
the curiosity that started this madness.

That clip is the ultimate pornography.

It has tainted my mistress, the night.

What used to be the most beautiful time for me is now the
most threatening.

I no longer recognize the night as a friend.

I long for the sunlight instead.

I long for dawn and the daylit hours that follow.

I long to erase these images from my head.

To wash them out with sunlight.

Some days I think they will soon be gone.

But then when night falls again, and the blackness reaches its
prime in the hours after midnight, I realize they are still there
and even more powerful than before.

VI.

The face goes slack after the head is severed. The muscles
are at rest, but it's only been seconds since the eyes have

glazed over. The mouth hangs open. The head is resisting gravity. It is dangled by its hair and becomes an object hanging in the air.

There's this myth that the eyes can still see for a moment after a decapitation. The eyes can still see after the head is no longer attached to the body. I imagine those eyes still being able to see. Those eyes are glaring right at me through the darkness from across the room. Those eyes are my eyes in my reflection whenever I pass by a mirror in the blackness of night.

VII.

If only I could stop scaring myself.

I see the head everywhere at night now and when I peer down the darkened hall, shivers go up my spine. I see shapes in the dark that I never saw before and I can't not see them. I'm convinced they are there. There's still a severed head somewhere in this house. When I pass by a mirror I try not to look in my own eyes for fear of seeing my head as a severed head: a head removed from its body. The severed head might be under the bed because I feel a presence from under there sometimes and I don't dare look to confirm it. For I know it's all open space and blackness under there and if I could will myself to peek my eyes would surely catch the glimmer of a dead set of eyes — the eyes of a severed head staring back at me.

VIII.

Where will I find the head? Surely in the darkest place imaginable and in my most alone moment in the terribly fearful night it will finally take tangible form. Will the head be my own, I wonder? Or maybe the head of someone I love? Or maybe *his* head — the head of the man I watched die?

IX.

I will stand in the darkened room as a dare and stare into the eyes of my own reflection.

Since this all began as a dare, it can end as a dare too . . .
But I cannot even begin to go.
And I think I just heard a noise.
Oh God let me remove these bed covers and see what it is.
Jesus. The face is staring at me from across the room.
The eyes are staring at me from the closet
The glimmer of the dead eyes
The eyes of a deceased decapitated head
The loose muscles of the jaw
Slackened human face
Inhuman eyes
Unreal but really there staring across at me
Let the sun come up. Let it rise to vanquish the blackness of this night, a night that has lasted a lifetime—nine full nights!
Merciful God, this is my plea:
I am sorry I watched that clip!
Let the light return to the space behind my eyes!

CASE #:93436

JESUS FUCK; OR, THE BEHEADING
BY JAY HELMSTUTLER

Jay Helmstutler holds an M.F.A. in Creative Writing from American University in Washington, D.C., and has an unpublished collection of dark fiction under his belt.

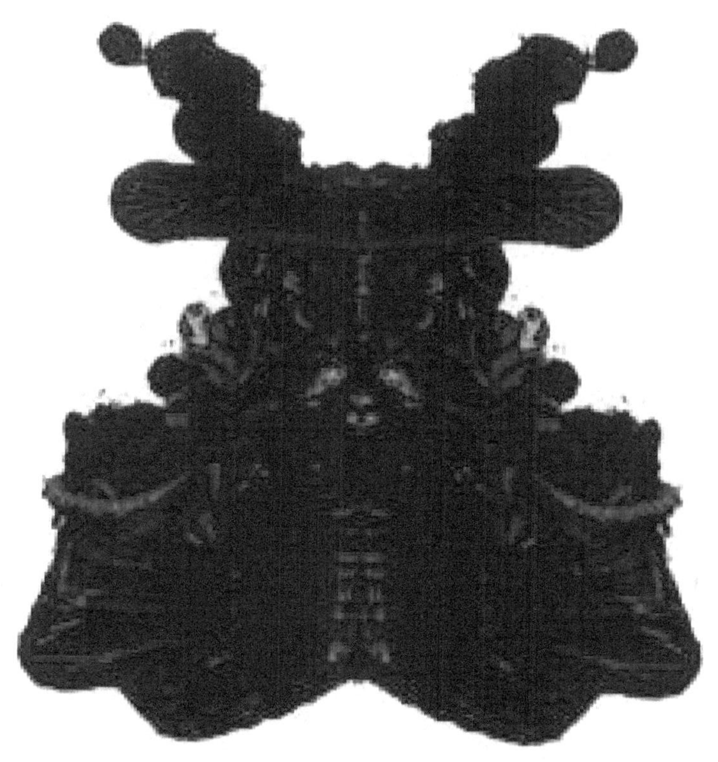

Exoskeleton by Martin Ian Smith

SHILOH SNIFFED THE GROUND AND BARKED LIKE A DOG. She circled. She squatted over the dirt and shit beside the apple tree that shaded thesmall graves in front of the farmhouse. Her hair had grown out since master had last cut it. It tickled her eye and she shook her head from side to side. Shiloh's restraints felt cold against the sweat on her skin as she lapped water from the pond.

Shiloh caught her reflection in a gap in the pond's skin of dead leaves. A gaunt face stared back at her with dark eyes, a misshapen nose and sharp shoulder-blades hunched up behind. It didn't register as dog. It didn't register as human. She saw Shiloh.

Good Shiloh.

A leather collar, worn and stretched and twisted from the early days when whoever Shiloh used to be had objected to it, hung loose around her neck and from it hung a steel tag which confirmed her Shilohness. Chains looped under the collar and formed a thick web with others that spread across her naked back that was pink with brown scratches and bruises from the harsh irons and master's temper. The chains bled into bent steel poles that curved with her torso to form an external ribcage. Draped in iron and steel, Shiloh stood on her elbows and knees and drank. When she dreamed, Shiloh dreamed as a dog dreams, of running, of chasing, of jumping. Sometimes she dreamed that she still had her hands and feet. The air beyond her stumps often itched and she would want to lick herself there, but there was nothing to lick.

Shiloh turned away from the creature in the water and saw master watching her. He stood at the back door in a sweat-stained polo shirt and piss-stained pants, filling the frame with his square shoulders and frowning through his wiry beard. He held something that looked like knives in his upturned palms.

Master called Shiloh over: "Tud yma!"

She didn't speak Welsh – Shiloh hadn't spoken a word in any language for six months and couldn't call one to mind if she tried – but she understood him well enough now to avoid another night in the coal bunker.

Shiloh moved slow and loud, clinking with every hard-won step towards the greystone farmhouse thick with dead wall-crawlers, and she pulled herself up into the kitchen.

"Eisteddwch," master said, kneeling, and Shiloh sat.

He asked for her paw and she put her right stump into his large left hand. The skin at the end of her arm had twisted in the healing. It was not a clean cut. The girl who entered the farmhouse that day had nearly bled out. Shiloh was nearly lost before she had even been formed. But master was more resourceful than he looked and he kept her going through the blood loss and a severe infection that came later. Once the girl lost her hands and feet – a gradual process in which she was dismantled one piece at a time over the course of many months – it took only a few simple pushes for her to lose herself, too. Master petted the tight, warped skin at the juncture where her hand should have started and placed the knife blades, which were welded onto a circular steel band over a rough sack, onto her stump, creating a set of six-inch claws.

Shiloh took back her stump and placed it on the ground. The new claw clicked on the once-white tiles. The band ate into her flesh. She whimpered and squirmed and scraped the claw against the floor to pull it off. Master pushed it back on and shouted his disapproval. He grabbed a hammer and Shiloh made herself small. When master placed an identical claw on her left stump, Shiloh understood that it belonged there. It was to be part of her Shilohness.

Master repeated a single phrase as he tightened the claws and washed Shiloh down with a flannel; it crept out over and over through master's murmered, half-English-half-Welsh sentences and stuck in Shiloh's head, though she didn't fully understand its meaning.

Dog show.

***

The car frightened Shiloh. She lay in the boot in the dark. The boot was lined with plastic. She licked it. Her stomach gargled. Her diet had been reduced in the last two days: a bowl of biscuits in the morning and a chew toy after master's games in the garden. Shiloh had learned to bite and jump and slash with her new claws. No hay bale or log was safe. A week ago master had let her kill a rabbit with her teeth. Shiloh remembered nothing from before her life on the farm, but the rabbit's blood was warm and metallic and more exciting than anything she could imagine. She thought about the rabbit as she curled up with her eyes wide open in the dark.

The car stopped. The afternoon sun blinded her. Master attached a lead to her new collar. Both were red. Shiloh climbed down with a little help and was dragged along by her neck before her eyes could adjust. The edge of the collar dug in beneath her chin. Master used his firm voice. Shiloh heard other voices, other firm voices, masculine and impatient.

Ysgol y Fan Fach closed ten years ago, but it had not forgotten its children. Their swings still hung, creaking on a rusted frame. Their drawings still fluttered on the walls: horses; beaches; mam a dad a fi in crayon. The glass around the back of the building, in the window overlooking the playground and the cloud-veiled mountains beyond, still held a dozen small hand-prints in red and white and green paint. Shiloh fought against the lead for a better look at the hand-prints. She pulled and master stopped and the lead was taut for a moment. In that moment, she took in the lines and the cracks of the hands and the spots where the paint had squashed under too much pressure. Cold impressions of such warm moments marked the building throughout and the glimpses of happiness weighed as heavy on Shiloh as the metal on her back. In the happiness, there was a distant feeling of familiarity. She could almost feel the touch of paint on her own phantom hands, but she couldn't imagine when or where or why master would have allowed her to do it.

The moment passed.

Shiloh's crude exoskeleton clicked and clacked all the way into the assembly hall. The chains bounced off the ribs and the claws knocked on the half-rotten flooring. Shiloh froze at the entrance between the moss-covered doors which dangled from their hinges. The hall was full of masters and Shilohs.

Good Shiloh.

Master pulled her inside and towards the back wall, near a decrepit piano and under a small, rotting Jesus on the other side of the wire-fence circle in the centre of the hall. She looked at the damp, splintered Jesus, his body full of woodworm, and snuggled her head next to master's leg.

The other Shilohs didn't answer to Shiloh. They answered to Toto, to Chance, to Laika and to Shep. The one Shiloh tried not to look at as the masters talked, as they prodded and petted each other's nervous possessions, he had long hair covering his face with bright eyes piercing through as he twitched his head to take everything in. This one was called Buck. He was taller than Shiloh. He still had his hands and feet. All but Shiloh did, and the other masters were very interested in the stumps under her claws. Buck's claws were made of old screws. They stuck out from his knuckles, seven or eight per fist, wrapped in dirty bandages and leather strips. Other dogs had claws too and were intimidating in their own way – Chance had a metal frame around his jaw with blades jutting from his mouth to create a second set of teeth – but Buck was different, held himself differently. The dogs were starved and frail, all except Buck. Buck was a muscular kind of thin, the youngest of them all, and he looked like he had been a dog most of his life; his arms and legs had developed just right for crawling and making small lunging leaps to hunt or to greet master at the door. Buck, out of all the starved, sweaty, frightened dogs, was the only one who moved and acted as if life on all-fours was his intended state. However much the others tried and believed with all their hearts, they were always hindered and confused by the pain and the clumsiness of their existence. When Buck looked at the other dogs, his lips twisted into a silent snarl. Buck snarled in Shiloh's direction, hunched at his master's feet, and Shiloh saw that his teeth had been filed into imperfect fangs, some cracked and some left as broken shards. Shiloh didn't snarl back. She tucked her head closer against master's leg.

Good Shiloh.

The dogs were chained to makeshift hooks the oldest master, the one they called Tudor, had hammered into the walls. The masters were all old, all men, most with greying moustaches, but Tudor seemed to command their attention despite being the smallest and leanest. Shiloh watched as he took a plastic camera from another man's hand and smashed it under his boot-heel. The man, the owner of the one called Laika, was upset about his camera, but despite being twice the size of Tudor he retired to the corner without further protest. The masters spoke and admired each other's work. They took out their flasks of tea and plastic-wrapped biscuits. Shiloh's master was patted on the back and had his hand shaken by everyone who saw her. They called him by his name – master's name was Jala – and touched Shiloh and used words like 'beautiful' and 'bendigedig'.

'Deww, she is a stunner,' Tudor said, a hand on his Toto's shaved head. Jala smiled as Tudor left and began addressing all the masters. Shiloh saw her master's smile drop and she met his eyes. Jala tousled her hair and looked away.

'Good Shiloh,' he said, adjusting his crotch. 'Don't you worry now.'

The girl Shiloh used to be was screaming. Her hands and feet ached, heavy with stalled blood. The old wood scratched her back as she bucked to loosen her restraints. Bound to a table in an X position, her arms and legs were roped at each corner. 'Don't you worry now. Be good. Be quiet. No-one can hear. No-one but us. We're all alone out here, cariad.' All she could see was ceiling. All she could say was 'God'.

A word almost formed on Shiloh's lips. A name.

Jala knelt beside Shiloh as Chance was pulled past them away from Laika who he had tried to pin. Jala looked into his dog's eyes and asked a soft question. He wiped away a tear she didn't know was there with his big hand and kissed her on the forehead. His beard tickled her nose.

A much younger girl slapped her painted hand down on paper. Her mother high-fived her. Mother's hand was much bigger than her own. 'Don't worry, sweetheart. You'll grow.' Mother kissed her on the forehead.

The word came to Shiloh's lips again, but fell away before she could get it out. A name.

Jala studied her closely. She could feel his gaze and lifted her head. Their eyes met. His brown. Hers blue. The brown searched the blue for an explanation. The blue looked away.

Shiloh licked her master's hand and tried to wag a tail that didn't exist.

After an hour, the chatter and the giddiness that came with showing off their pets had died away. The masters had run out of words. They looked at one another for some kind of signal. They looked to Tudor. He unveiled a small, silver-coloured trophy: a plastic, jumping dog on a plastic, burgundy base. Tudor spoke to the masters who nodded and chuckled in places that made Tudor show his five-toothed smile. Shiloh understood some of the words: 'dogs' and 'hungry' and 'fucking', which was every other word for the masters in the hall. Shiloh shivered at the touch of the metal exoskeleton on her skin as she shuffled on her elbows and knees. The other dogs were naked too, all but Laika. Shiloh could smell the fear leaking from Laika's fur one-piece. It spread across the floor and Shiloh shifted her claws away from it. She met Laika's eyes. Laika did not look away first.

A word Shiloh did not understand was said almost as much as 'fucking', and it soon it would be almost all anyone said. Chance and Shep were led by their masters into the wire-fence circle. The fence was hooked back into place.

All anyone could say now was 'kill'.

***

The pale afternoon became a breezy evening by camping lights – the wind entered through cobwebs littered with flies – and the floor, once brittle underfoot and prone to cracking sounds, was soggy and squelched with blood and piss. Shiloh gritted her teeth and shut her eyes to block out the sounds that came from the circle.

Chance and Shep were the first to fight. It began with much barking and growling. Shep was the oldest of the dogs at thirty-something years old, and the most loving. His baby-blue eyes would look nowhere but at his master. He would lick at his hand and try to lick his face at every opportunity. Shep's unique losses – there was a deformed mound of skin between his legs where his testicles had been removed and his scrotum sewn up against his crotch – drew almost as much attention as Shiloh's missing hands and feet. As the masters poked and prodded at his emptiness, Shep wiggled his behind and smiled, his mouth always open with his tongue slack between his jaws. Shep smiled like that right until they led him into the circle. He trotted in with black boxing gloves on his hands wrapped in barbed wire. He didn't look away from his master until Chance had sunk his metal mouth-piece into his arm.

After first blood was drawn, the fight became a silent one. The dogs circled one another on all-fours. Shep stole worried glances at his master that were met with his shout of "Kill!"

Before Shep could do any such thing, Chance pinned him to the floor and penetrated his throat with his metal second-teeth, so far down that Chance also sank his first-teeth into Shep's shredded flesh.

The fight became a noisy one again.

Shep made not even the slightest pretense of a howl or a yelp. Shep screamed. Shep screamed until his last breath. And his master was disappointed.

The scream cut Shiloh to the bone.

Red on white. The farmhouse was cold, but the girl was soaked in sweat. Skull and brain on walls. Nowhere to hide.

Shiloh opened her eyes and the images remained. Nowhere to hide. A bloodied blue tie. A man's skull came back together as the fire re-entered the shotgun and word formed on his lips. It was a name.

Shiloh shook her head free of it. Her left claw pinched the skin around her stump, but that is where it belonged.

Jala helped Shep's master drag Shep's heavy body out of the hall and through the far door. Shep twitched and bled – the snail-trail of slick, dark blood in his wake left a path for the next loser to follow – and he was placed out of sight. Shiloh crept forward to peer through the door after him, but the lead around her neck drew tight. The hook gave somewhat. Shiloh watched it bend as she pulled. Pieces of Shep's silent death scream, lit with crumbs of gaslight that reached from the hall, gazed back at Shiloh.

The girl on the table screamed and pulled at the binding around her right arm in the sliver of sunlight through the narrow windows. She clenched her fist and pulled hard, crying, begging, saying that word 'God'. A man came in. It was her master, but she didn't call him master. Not yet. He was something else. She called him what he was and he beat her. She called herself what she was. A name. The skull and brains man came back together with a flash and told her to run and called her what she was.

'Run, Eleri!' the face said.

The girl was an Eleri.

The Eleri shouted her Eleriness at the man who became her master. Over time, her Eleriness got her beatings and starvation and no sleep and no blanket and no sunshine and no right hand and no left hand and no right foot and no left foot. Finally, then, when her Eleriness could earn her no more punishments short of death, an Eleri became a Shiloh.

Toto and Buck were summoned to the circle. Toto refused. His eyes, wide and slick with tears, saw only the trail of blood on the floor that he was being asked to cross. Buck followed his master into the circle and sniffed around. He licked at Shep's blood and decided he liked it. His master, a weasel in overlarge reading glasses, giggled and petted his monstrosity. Buck looked up. He stood on his knees and palms, his arms straight and his dick hard between his legs. A blood-smeared snarl greeted Toto as he was dragged by his collar into the circle. Buck barked and bounced and waited to feed.

Toto wailed and fought, and then Toto stood up on his hind legs and tried to run.

"P-please!" he said. It began as a word and turned into a scream as the masters leaped towards him. They grabbed him by his limbs and held him down as his master begged for mercy.

"He's only new!" Toto's master said. "Give him time! Tudor, please!"

A piece of Eleri came back from the farmhouse and she and Shiloh backed against the wall and watched in horror as Toto thrashed and bled under a dozen hands.

Toto began to speak again. Shiloh watched as Jala grabbed him by the head and slammed it down into the floor. A fury overcame her master like she had never seen. He punched and kicked Toto in the head. Toto swallowed pieces of teeth and pints of blood and tried to beg. Tudor pushed the masters aside with the barrel of his shotgun. Toto's master left the hall. Through the silence, Shiloh heard a car start and leave at speed. Toto's breathing became sobs, wordless begging on his back as his arm reached all around for something to hold.

Jala watched his Shiloh as Tudor stood over the downed Toto.

Toto couldn't speak to beg and when he began to choke on his own blood his face was punched through by a shotgun blast, shattering the wooden floor on the other side of his skull. Shiloh was sprayed with a fine, warm mist. Through the mist, her master approached. Jala kneeled beside her and scratched her behind the ear. It didn't stop her from trembling.

"You have to fight, cariad" Jala said to her. "You're the best dog in this room. You're the best dog I ever had."

Shiloh tilted her head as he scratched her. She closed her eyes. Master's words landed inside her head. She replayed them. She understood them all.

Shiloh found herself back at the farmhouse with Eleri. Eleri stood outside the door. She knocked on the door with her hands and stood balanced on her feet. Beside her stood a man, the owner of the brains on the walls who had called her Eleri. He told her to knock again. In her white shirt and black cardigan and knee-high socks, Eleri asked why. She was told again to knock and Shiloh stepped into Eleri and did as she was told.

Eleri's father sat beside her on the threadbare sofa with bath towels for throw covers and asked the ox of a man sat opposite a question: 'Are you waiting for Christ to return?' Jala slurped at his tea and said he never thought about things like that. 'All that stuff,' he said, 'I don't have it in me.' Eleri's father sipped his tea and Eleri tried not to look at stacks of decade-old newspapers, slumped and faded photographs of horses in rotten frames, and a shocked-looking stuffed fox with no tail.

'It's never too late,' Eleri's father said, 'for the truth. Many people aren't given the gift of faith. It comes later. It's a lot of work, for some. My wife and I, Jesus found us pretty late on.'

Eleri looked at the fox and Jala noticed.

'It was right before we had Eleri, here,' Eleri's father said, 'so this lucky lady's never known an unhappy day in her life.'

Eleri looked at the pitiful picture of the once-proud horse as it stood alone in black and white and stains of yellow with its coat shining in the sun. She wondered where the horse was now and if horses are buried when they die.

'Can you take out some literature for this gentleman, Eleri?'

Are they buried with other horses in mass graves? Is the grave marked? Are words said when the horses are lowered into the dirt? Look at its face. Was it happy? Do horses feel happiness? I'd like to touch its coat. I wish it was still alive so I could feed it and make it like me. I wonder where its bones are.

'Eleri?'

'I'm sorry, dad.'

Eleri took out some leaflets, 'The Dead Can Live Again' and 'An End to Suffering' with painted portraits of Jesus and picnics and rainbow-backdrops, and handed them to her father.

'We can just leave these here, if you like,' he said. 'Maybe you don't read them right away, maybe you don't ever read them, but they're here if the time comes.'

Eleri sipped her sickly-sweet tea and looked at the wall. She could feel his eyes on her. She could sense the reason for his silence.

Eleri's dad laughed and put the leaflets on the coffee table between them and said, 'It's not as scary as all that, anyway. We've made quite a trip today, but if you ever have any questions, you can write to us. I'll just pop a card in with our address. Anything at all.'

Jala left the room. His eyes locked onto Eleri's for a moment as he exited into the kitchen. Eleri asked if they could leave. She felt a panic bubbling up beneath her skin. She couldn't look at this man any more. She couldn't allow him to look at her, this man who lived with dead foxes and dead horses and newspapers written by dead people. She asked again if they could leave. The skull and brains said no until the skull and the brains saw a shotgun. Throwing himself across Eleri, the skull and the brains screamed for her to run and then vanished into fine, warm mist.

'Eleri, run!'

***

Laika waited in the ring-fence circle. She wore a blue, felt onesie with a white belly and a hole at the back. A damp, felt tail hung over the hole. When she turned, her sharp ribs poked at the sides. When she bent, the ridges of her vertebrae and shoulder-blades tented the fabric. Starved and weak and afraid and with a face full of big, green eyes looking for help and the strength to trick herself into believing it might come, Laika was a spinosaurus in blue. Her long blonde hair was black with blood at the tips, dipped in Shep's death, and her face, designed with nothing of the rigidity of a dog's which can express little more than vague happiness or extreme aggression, was a picture of fear. Her pink mouth was turned down at the corners and her lips trembled as much as her hands did when she crawled to the farthest edge of the circle from the entrance. Eleri entered the circle. Shiloh waited for her outside the circle. She awaited Eleri's decision.

Laika's eyes stopped their search for help and locked onto the handless and footless, short-haired girl perched opposite. Eleri clinked and clacked a few more steps inside the circle, her elbows sliding on the blood. Jala padlocked the fence back in place and handed the key to Tudor, who patted him on the shoulder. Jala bowed his head for two breaths and with renewed enthusiasm turned back towards the circle where his Franken-friend was locked in a fearful stare with Laika, the undisputed amateurish runt of the hall.

Laika's knuckles were white as she strangled the small piece of iron that held together her three four-inch blades on each hand that poked between her slim fingers.

'Kill the bitch!' Jala said. 'Do her, Shiloh! Kill!'

Laika looked at Jala and then at Eleri. Eleri knew then that Laika understood the masters' words, just as she now did. Eleri had been trained and beaten and operated on and burnt down and rebuilt as Shiloh, so her understanding, spurred on by a simple painted hand on a window, needed to be dragged out from the deepest, darkest, safest hiding place in her mind. One look at Laika told Eleri that she had always understood. This was not a dog, had never been a dog; this was a person still on the road to complete breakdown. She had suffered, but she was stronger than Eleri.

Laika moved her mouth and spoke under the masters' cries for her death. Eleri frowned. She could hear nothing but garbled pleas for violence that pressed down on her from all sides, so she moved forwards. Laika backed against the wire fence and was kicked away from it by a heavy boot from the other side.

Eleri moved closer, feeling her claws sticking to the wooden floor. She moved slow.

Jala allowed himself a smile as his Shiloh beared down, however cautiously, on the now frantic, sobbing Laika.

Laika held her right claw out in front of her. She was talking, but Eleri couldn't hear. She moved closer and was now almost within Laika's clawing range. Words came through. Words like 'no' and 'please' and 'wait' and 'wait' and 'please' and 'Eleri'.

Tudor brought up his shotgun and, with both dogs looking, slid two new shells into the barrel. Jala shook his head at Tudor. Tudor snapped the shotgun shut and the sound quietened the hall.

Laika lowered her trembling claw and spoke through her trembling lips: 'Eleri, please. Please don't, Eleri. Please. It's me. It's me.'

'Wait in the car,' Eleri's father said. 'We won't be long.' 'Why do I have to go in?' Eleri said. 'I've been into three houses in a row!'

Eleri's sister, Gwennan, stuck out a tongue and went back to her Nintendo.

'Don't you know me?' said Gwennan, the spinosaurus in blue. 'Don't you remember who I am?'

'I fuckin' told you this was a bad idea,' Tudor said, pushing Laika's master. 'You're too fuckin' soft! We let you in and you fuckin' let us down! If you'd have spent as much time training her as you did fuckin' her, she'd be fuckin' perfect!'

Tudor swung his gun around at Laika's master who ducked behind another master and held up his hands and cried out.

A tear fell from Eleri's eye. She felt it trace a line down her cheek. Eleri had a plan and was already five steps down the line with Gwennan driving the car as best she could, with the masters killing one another at the school as they fled to safety, to their home, to their mother, to their future together. It was hard for Eleri. Her mother and Gwennan had to help her with everything at first and, despite everything, there were moments of frustration and harsh words were said. But they were always taken back. Nothing could be worse than the masters and what little bit of life they had managed to recover after their nightmares was to be cherished and never taken for granted.

Doctors came to Eleri's aid and gave her back her feet and basic versions of her hands. Now and again, as Gwennan tenderly slotted Eleri's hands onto her arms, Eleri would think of master's steel claws. She would cry and cry, but it would stop. Gwennan would cry sometimes too, but, again, it would stop. They had each other. The masters were all dead or in prison. There was only mam, Gwennan, Eleri and God, who had brought them back together, who had saved them where their frail, human father had failed.

Eleri struck first. Gwennan recoiled and screamed, pushing down the flaps of skin on her blood-soaked face. The blood startled Eleri and she almost stopped, but she fought through the shock and hit her again. Gwennan fell to the floor as the muscles in her arm split under the steel claws, painting them black. The third strike took a long time to come. Gwennan's claws lay on the floor and her bare hands shielded her face. Eleri scrambled on top of her sister and stood on her hands and knees over her, their bodies touching as Gwennan writhed in agony and the kind of terror that comes once in a lifetime, at the end. Everyone watched. The third strike had to convince them of her Shilohness. There was no future for an Eleri in this place. The masters are not people you escape from. Once they have you, they have you. They take your hands and your feet and the best you can hope for is to please them well enough that they don't take anything else.

Eleri pinned Gwennan's wrists to the floor with her claws either side of her screeching head, crucifying her manic sister. There was no more talk. There would be no more fantasies, no more memories. Eleri crawled back inside herself to hide. Shiloh wagged her tail and lept with glee into the ring. Eleri found a recess of her mind where no-one would ever find her again. Shiloh barked. Shiloh howled. Gwennan had never been a dog, and now she was no longer human. She had lost the ability to think and speak and became a bag of pain trying to escape itself with its bleeding wrists pinned to the floor and its neck exposed.

Shiloh remembered nothing from before her life on the farm, but Gwennan's blood was warm and metallic and more exciting than anything she could imagine. It filled her mouth and exploded over her face. The fear that slipped from Gwennan's expression was absorbed and turned into joy in Shiloh's. As Gwennan was dragged gurgling and spluttering into death, Shiloh found new life. Eleri couldn't look her sister in the eyes. Shiloh entered and took in every delicious detail of her kill, from its fingernails scratching at the floor to the wiggling of its tongue in its wide, ugly mouth.

The hall fell silent but for Shiloh's panting and Gwennan's bleeding. As Gwennan died, so Eleri faded.

Tudor lowered his shotgun and grinned at Shiloh.

***

The trophy was given a home on Jala's mantlepiece. The plastic dog lept from his plastic base for many years. Shiloh never again heard the words 'dog show' and never found out what became of the other masters and the other Shilohs, Buck and Chance. She was unusually quiet and withdrawn for some time after the dog show, but master kept her in treats and let her sleep in front of the fire and soon enough she was back to her old self; life returned to baths and walks and treats and curling up at her master's feet through the winters.

There were times when Shiloh would find herself staring into space for no reason. She would sit in the garden and gaze at the sun going down behind the mountains and her mind would quieten. The quiet made Shiloh nervous. It was as if she was listening for something, but she didn't know what.

Many baths and many walks and many treats passed, and Shiloh's hair was greying and master had long ago made pads to support her stiffening elbows and knees. Shiloh had forgotten all about the dog show. It was at this time sickness came to master's house. He would sleep more, spend more time in the bathroom, eat less and smiles were harder won. Shiloh doted on him as the weight fell away from his body. In the weeks before his death, the walks and the meals became more infrequent as master's strength left him.

When master lay in his bed and refused to speak any more, Shiloh couldn't understand. When he didn't wake up to fill her bowl with biscuits or tuna or leftovers, Shiloh was confused. She sat by his side as often as possible and, unable to open the door, used the kitchen to shit and piss in. Shiloh often looked at the door and scratched at it with her stump. Once, that would have been enough to raise master to open the door. Now, nothing would raise him. He turned grey at first, then a shade of green. By the time he turned brown, the stench had driven Shiloh from the room. She slept downstairs in front of the unlit fire and dreamed of times when it would warm her body. She chose a new room to shit and piss in and stayed away from the kitchen.

The silence frightened Shiloh more than the hunger. She found herself listening again. She was waiting for someone to speak – she didn't know who – but a voice never came.

However much the silence frightened Shiloh, though, it was the hunger that killed her.

The End

107

CASE #61426

EXOSKELETON

BY MARTIN IAN SMITH

Martin is a postgraduate student at Aberystwyth University, Wales, and self-publishes horror comics, such as The Watchful Sea and A Rope Around Your Broken Neck, which are housed over at Attackosaur.com.

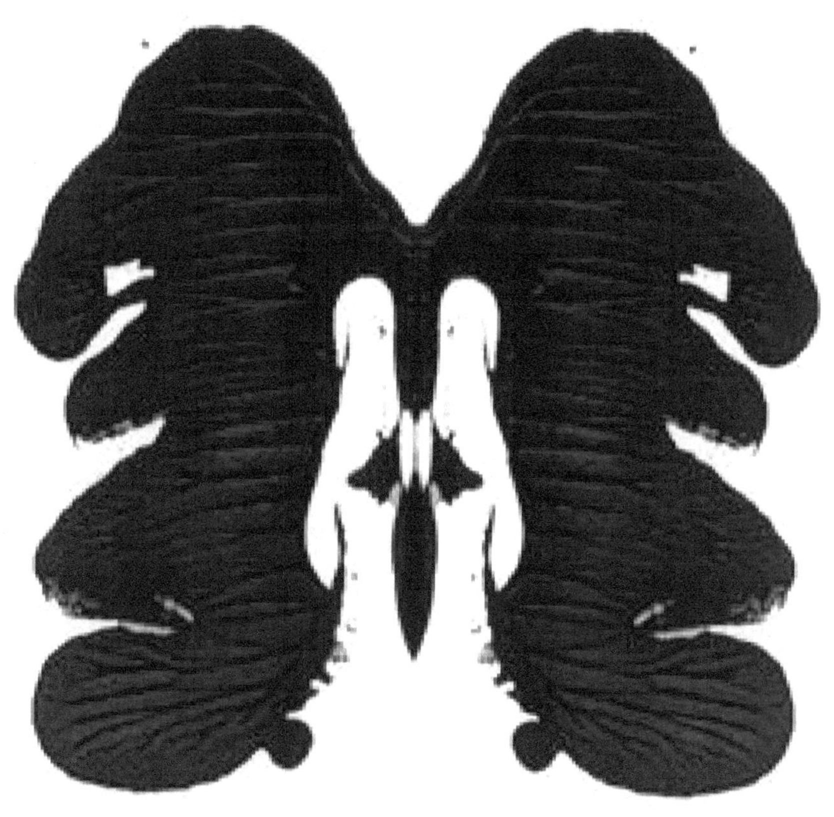

Cemetery Dead Ahead by Leonard J. Dawson

STANDING ALL BY MYSELF NEXT TO MY UNCLE'S OPEN COFFIN, I almost screamed when that one cloudy eye of his popped open and looked right at me as if he'd been lying in there playing dead, waiting for me to get close so he could frighten me.

All the kids called him "Old One-Eye" because he wore a patch over one eye, just like a pirate. And his good eye was so cloudy it was almost white. And they were all as scared of him as I was.

Then his thin white lips whispered, "Come here, Davy," and I ran away, pushing and shoving my way through the crowd at his wake, running as though my dead uncle had climbed out of that coffin to chase me. And when I got outside I ran some more, and I didn't stop running for a long, long time.

I guess folks were in a hurry to get rid of him because they put him in the ground later that same day. I probably should've told someone he wasn't really dead, but I didn't because I wanted him buried so he couldn't ever look at me with that scary eyeball again.

I didn't go to the burial service, and not just because the crazy old coot had scared me. I didn't want to miss out on Trick or Treat. Yeah, that's right, my uncle died on Halloween. Halloween's no different from any other day when it comes to dying. So by the time they were putting sod over him a couple of hours later, the night was full of little ghouls and goblins collecting candy, the streetlights turning them into long, spider-thin, wildly-animated shadows slithering about the neighborhood.

The other kids shied away from me because mine was the scariest costume of all. One woman who opened the door to greet me even yelled to someone in the house, "Jesus, Harry, you gotta come see this kid's costume."

Another lady handing out candy just stood there with her mouth open after she saw me. When I reached into her bowl I said, "Boo," because I thought it'd be fun to make her scream. It wasn't. My ears rang from her shriek.

My bag was nearly full of candy when I spotted them half a block away, a gang of older boys standing around a little kid wearing a Superman costume, six of them, and all of them bigger and older than me. They looked kinda familiar, but then bullies all look alike, don't they?

One of them said something to the kid I couldn't hear. The little guy held his bag of candy behind his back then stuck his chin out defiantly and shook his head. Brave little guy; stupid too, and I already know what you're thinkin' - that I should've gone and helped him. Well, I've had my turn getting beat up. Now I'm smarter than that. And besides, how else is he gonna learn?

I watched them take the kid's bag of candy and push him to the ground, but I didn't stick around to see what they did to him next because one of them spotted me. He pointed at me and yelled, "Hey, look, it's that same kid from last year."

I turned around and ran away as fast as I could, as fast as I ran when my uncle scared me at the wake. And when I looked back over my shoulder they were coming after me. I can run really fast for my age, but those boys were bigger and their legs were longer.

I should've run to the nearest house where they were giving out candy, but I panicked, cutting across someone's lawn, running between two houses and through some shrubs. Then I rolled under an iron fence into the cemetery. I'd had the wild idea that I could hide there in the darkness, but as soon as I cleared that fence I felt the despair that sets in when you realize you've made a really bad decision you can't undo.

I headed for the mausoleums deep in the cemetery, beyond even the faintest glow of the streetlights. It would be dark there, as dark as any place on this earth ever gets, and the gravestones would be bigger, big enough to hide behind, if I could make it that far before those boys caught me.

I ran till my sides ached then stopped to catch my breath, leaning over to put my hands on my knees. Looking back, I saw six dark shapes backlit by far-off street lights spread out into a line that soon became an arc, the boys at the sides running the fastest, forming a semi-circle that would soon close around me. I couldn't outrun them but I ran anyway, trying to outrun the thought of what they'd do to me when they caught me, but how do you outrun what's in your head? And I knew they'd be extra mad when they caught me because I'd made them chase me. And there wasn't anyone around to stop them from beating me to a ragged, bloody pulp.

Why I thought of my bag of candy then I don't know, but I realized I didn't have it anymore and I couldn't remember when I'd dropped it. But I forgot all about my candy when those boys began to threaten me, yelling things like, "Hey, kid. You know what I'm gonna do to you? I'm gonna shove sticks in your eyes when I catch you," and, "We're gonna dig up a fresh grave and put you in with the stiff and cover you up with dirt."

I ran again, as fast as I could, swerving around the gravestones like a slalom skier. I caught glimpses of the shadowy figures running off to the sides, bullies closing the circle around me. In a few seconds I'd have to stop or I'd run right into them, and my back prickled with the expectation that at any moment hands would grab me from behind.

"There you are," someone yelled as I swerved around a large headstone, a blast of frosty air hitting me, as though the cry echoing off the gravestones around me had come to me on a North Wind. I slid to a stop on the grass, almost crashing into Old One-Eye and coming to a stop right in front of him.

I heard a collective gasp behind me. It was the bullies. They had me trapped, but I didn't dare take my eyes off the specter in front of me - Old One-Eye, wild-eyed and grinning like the crazy man people said he was.

I'd forgotten they'd buried him in that cemetery or I never would've cut through there. I wondered what a man who'd been buried alive would do to the kid who hadn't said anything, the kid who'd let them put him in the ground and cover him with dirt, but the crazy old coot seemed more interested in something behind me, so I spun around to see what he was looking at.

Turned out those tough kids weren't so tough after all. They were backing away from Old One-Eye. Then one of them broke and ran and they all scattered, the six of them running away in six different directions, running like the devil himself was after them. I saw a patch of moonlight twinkle in Old One-Eye's cloudy eyeball as he watched them run away.

Grinning like a lunatic, he yelled at them. "I'll show you what I do to bullies."

With the bullies gone and my uncle taking no notice of me, I decided to run for it, but as I spun around to make my escape a boney hand closed on my shoulder like a vise. Old One-Eye turned me around to face a headstone that read, "Here lies Davy Bryant, age ten, taken from his loving parents before his time."

When I saw my name etched in that stone I felt a chill inside that went all the way down to my bones. Sometimes we just know something even though all of our senses let us down, the way I knew it was me under that stone. I looked down at my body then and I could see right through to my bones, my flesh thin and wispy as though it was made of nothing thicker than dirty bath water.

Pieces of broken memories flashed before me then; me running from those same bullies last Halloween, and the one before that, and the one before that. Then I saw Old One-eye jump out at me from behind a tree. I saw myself run into the street, felt a car slam into me. The last thing I saw was me lying in the street with One-eye standing over me and my candy scattered all over the road and the other kids going after it like crows on road kill.

That's when the images stopped. I thought about the bullies and being dead, and was bewildered by it all, so I asked Old One-Eye, "If I'm dead, how come people can see me?"

He told me I'd drift among the living until I had accepted my death; and that I'd keep reliving that night until I did.

When I asked him why he was still around, he trained that cloudy eye of his on me and said, "Your mother sent me to find you that night. When I saw you running from those bullies I jumped out from behind a tree and yelled, "Boo," to scare them away. But I frightened you too, and that's why you ran in front of the car that night. You've been stuck here reliving the past until I made amends. So after they buried me I stayed behind to protect you from those boys. We're gonna have some fun with them next time. I tried to tell you that when you were standing by my coffin at the funeral home."

Old One-eye didn't seem so scary after that. I was glad he was on my side of forever.

The End.

CASE #: 45669

CEMETERY DEAD AHEAD BY

LEONARD J. DAWSON

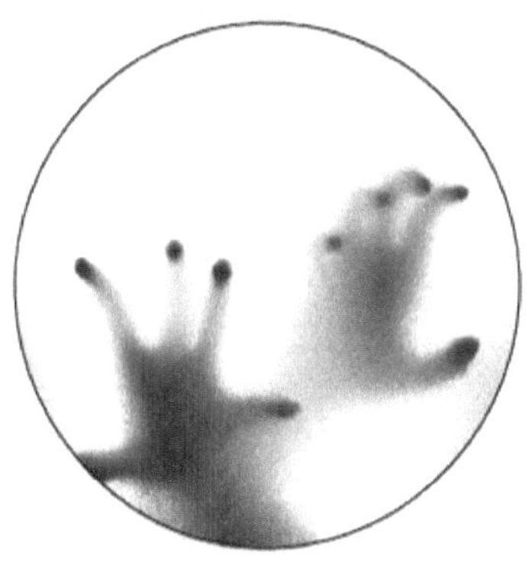

Details not released at this time

Stacy by Myles Paine

I was growing impatient. There I sat in that seedy hotel room, lounging comfortably in the worn-in suit I'd had on all day, just waiting. Waiting for her. Hoping it was all worth it.

Stacy.

She was beautiful. Blond hair like waves of mid-summer sunshine, legs from here to Bangkok. She was all I could think about since we'd met at that bar. Tailspin Tavern. More like Trouble Tavern. I'd never been there before and Stacy, a regular, knew. I arrived an outcast, like an alien landing down on the foreign wooden barstool, and she spotted the stranger from a mile a away the second I sat down. She said it's why she came up to me so fast, flirted with me until I gave in and bought her a drink.

A gin martini. I looked over at the bottle of Tanqueray waiting for her on the hotel dresser, then down at my watch. She was 15 minutes minutes late, and I stared at the second hand, watching it tick around until she was 16 minutes late. My nerves kicked in, a growing pit of shameful, but excited turmoil knotted up inside my stomach. I was supposed to be a married man. I knew it was wrong, but I didn't care. I'd searched so long for someone like Stacy, and I finally found her.

I stumbled out of my chair to the bathroom, as the bourbon I'd been sipping on started to weigh down my loafers. My steps were sloppy as I made my way to the sink. Turning on the faucet, I splashed the cool water on my face and looked at my reflection. I did well. This was the best I'd ever looked. My graying hair was freshly cropped short with a few strands resting carelessly to the side of my forehead. Careless, but planned, showing I wanted to look good, but didn't need to put in as much effort to do so.

My suit jacket dropped from my shoulders and I savored the feeling as the open air hit me, cooling my skin, flushed from the alcohol. I picked up my tumbler glass, gulped down another sip, and smiled.

I'd been drinking bourbon that night at the bar. The job, the wife, the kids, it was all getting to be too much. I needed the the break.

Needed the change.

I needed Stacy.

There was a knock on the door and I dropped my glass into the sink in surprise, the brown booze swishing over the side onto the floor. My chest fluttered and my heart fell, then rose in excitement as I realized she was there. I wasted no time getting to the door. I didn't even bother to check through the peephole to make sure someone else wasn't on the other side. The bellhop, a maid, maintenance, hell, even my wife. I knew Stacy was there. I felt it.

I swung open the door and saw her, beauty wrapped up tight in a tiny red dress, her white-blond hair flowing down her shoulders like a lion's mane. Her sultry blue eyes narrowed at me, closing in on her prey.

"Hey stranger," she said.

The sexy scratch in her voice blended with the bourbon in my bloodstream, coursing through my veins into my lustful heart. Oh, how I needed her.

"Come in," I said, stepping back from the door in invitation.

I couldn't bring myself to give a welcoming grin. My nerves and sexual longing took over, and all I could do was gape at her in desire.

Stacy sat elegantly down on the bed. I watched her legs cross and followed the smooth, tan skin down from her thighs to her seductive red shoes - her ruby slippers of sex. They were the same deep rouge as her dress and the heels went to eternity, ending in a small point, the tip sharp enough to kill a man. It turned me on more than I could bear.

"Sorry I'm late," She said, lighting up a thin white cigarette.

I glanced over at the no-smoking sign sitting on the table behind her bare shoulder, but said nothing. She didn't care. Why should I?

"Traffic was hell and my cab driver was an idiot. I think he was cracked out or something."

Stacy wasn't the smartest, but that didn't matter. I wasn't in this for the brain, just the body.

I took the cigarette, her delicate fingers not wanting to separate from the stick, and set it on the night table. She'd already kept me waiting long enough; I couldn't take it anymore. I climbed on her, pushing her back onto the hotel bed. She smiled and grazed her razor sharp nails along the back of my neck.

"Not wasting any time, huh?" said Stacy. "Fine by me."

The girl leaned up and touched her lips against mine. I gave in and kissed her, spreading her mouth open, exploring it with my tongue. I didn't give her too much, though. That's not what this was about.

I pulled away and gazed at her, hypnotizing her into a state of trance, of arousal and lust, until she was mine. I cupped her neck with a strong hand, not letting her break the stare. A few more seconds and confusion overwhelmed her. Her expression changed to fear for an instant, and then I was in her. Underneath, looking up at the man I used to be, moments before. Good god, he was heavy.

I pushed up, surprised at the strength in the girl's thin arms. The arms I now had complete control over. Stacy was mine. Finally.

The man flopped onto the bed, lifeless. He was still breathing, but wouldn't move or talk ever again. They never do when I leave them for someone new. No more kids, no more dealing with that grating god awful nag of a wife. I hoped Stacy had none of that. I was excited to learn her secrets.

I stood up from the bed and tried to walk, laughing as I wobbled on the 6-inch heels. I'd never worn them before. I'd never been a <u>woman</u> before. This was going to take some getting used to.

I made my way to the bathroom so I could see myself in the mirror. My hair was wild around my face. I pulled it back and held it in a ponytail, twisted it up into a bun, then wet my hands and slicked it back flat on my head. I gave myself a seductive, pouty look. It was everything, and I loved it.

I suddenly realized I felt a strange sensation, a weight on my chest I'd never felt before, and I looked down, noticing my breasts for the first time. I put a hand on each one, cupping and squeezing them through the thin red fabric. Spinning sideways to look at my profile, I grinned at my reflection and the curves that trailed down my body. Women were goddesses, and I was now one of the most decadent. I had to see myself in purest form.

Reaching a hand to my back, I struggled to find the zipper or latch or whatever was keeping the dress snug on my skin. I turned around, tried to face my back toward the mirror, tried to see what was holding the dress up, but it only hurt my neck from twisting sideways. Then I found it, barely catching the zipper between my thumb and forefinger. I slowly lowered my hand and dropped the dress from my body, breathing out a sigh of relief and satisfaction at the beauty that was unveiled. Stacy was perfect in every way. <u>I</u> was perfect.

I danced out of the bathroom, twirling around on my toes, my former shell watching me comatose from the bed. A loud banging on the hotel room door stopped my jubilation. Someone was knocking. Who?

I ran to the door and squinted through the peephole. A cop - uniform, hat, nightstick, and all - stood unamused on the other side.

Crap. What did he want?

Another persistent knock rattled the door and made my bare body flinch with growing dread. I started to get nervous, started taking deep breaths to keep calm. What was I supposed to do?

"Just a minute!" I said.

I picked up the used shell's legs and pulled forward, his upper body clunking onto the carpet as I dragged him off the bed. I took him to the bathroom and managed to shove him over the edge of the tub face first, and pulled the shower curtain to the side to hide him. A white towel hung from a hook next to the doorway. I grabbed it and wrapped the cloth around my body, then raced back to the waiting policeman. After easing the door back a few inches, I peered through the opening.

"Yes?" My nerves and confusion could be heard in the short greeting.

The cop threw out a hand and forced the door open completely. "Well?" he asked. "What happened?"

I took a step back into the room, trying to put some distance between me and my aggressor.

"What do you mean?"

"It's been a while," he said with a thick New York accent, looking behind my shoulder at the empty hotel room. "What happened to your trick?"

I didn't answer. Trick? What was this guy talking about?

The silence agitated him. He took a step forward, reclaiming his closeness to me, and raised his voice. "I asked you a question, slut." The cop gave me a heavy push and I tripped backwards. My feet came out from under me as I hit the bed, catching myself on my elbows. I lay there and watched him shut the door and begin stomping toward me. My mind reeled as I tried to come up with some sort of story to fix the situation. It's never easy when I first enter a new shell and have to learn about my new identity piece by piece, but I'd never had to deal with anything this intense before.

"He didn't show!" I finally called out. The officer stood still. "What? Why not?" "I don't know," I said.

"Well, what about my money?"

"Your money?"

He inched closer, his menacing brow narrowing in anger. "Don't play dumb, Stacy. You know the drill. I let you do your thing, work your corner, whore yourself out on Craigslist, whatever you need to make your dough, and I look the other way. For a fee.

"Would you rather me take you in for prostitution?"

I shook my head, too numb to answer. Realization ripped the words from my throat. This stupid whore. A prostitute.

The cop launched onto me, hands clamping tight on my neck. He was heavier than the last guy, and used his muscles to keep me pinned to the bed. I could feel their strength, their firmness, through his uniform.

"If you got no cash for me, I guess you'll have to make your payment another way."

All he could hear was a gargled whimper as I tried to choke out a response to make him stop. The officer tore off my towel, keeping one hand on my neck as he pawed at my exposed body with the other. He leaned into me and I felt his sticky, balmy breath on my throat, sending shivers of disgust through my soul. His arousal pressed against my thigh.

No.

I wasn't letting this happen. I wasn't being raped.

I struggled to knock the cop off of me, but he was a dead weight. He had me trapped against the scratchy blanket covering the bed, the fibers cutting into my flawless, feminine skin. For a second I thought of the man I was previously, that I'd left lifeless in this same spot just minutes earlier. Was that going to be me? Was this crooked creep going to leave me used and dead in this hotel, for the maids to dispose of?

I tried to shove harder, but it was no use. The officer's sweaty fingers forced my chin down, bringing his face to mine to look me straight in the eyes.

"Stop that," he said with a sneer. "You don't want to make this any more difficult than it needs to be. Just be good until I'm done with you."

Staring deep into his eyes, I lay still as a corpse.

Not on my watch, officer.

We didn't move. He was trapped in my gaze, and I became him. He wanted to enter me, but I penetrated him first. It took mere moments and then I was looking at her. Stacy. That gorgeous, troubled, naked girl, now useless to me.

I rolled off of her, sat on the edge of the bed, and ran a hand through my buzzed black hair, adjusting to the strength and power throbbing inside my new shell. My shirt and pants were snug on my muscles, and I could feel them gasping to be used. Adrenaline flashed through me. It wasn't natural. There was some substance flowing through my blood, pumping from my heart to my tingling fingernails. The hurricane of energy needed to be unleashed on something, anything.

Feeling around my uniform, I searched through the pockets until I found my police badge. I opened the wallet and read my new name: NYPD Police Officer Michael Gutierrez. I nodded, to no one in particular, just accepting the situation and thinking it through. A cop could be fun.

There were two bodies in this hotel room, though. Alive, but stripped of life, one with my new fingerprints all over it. I'd have to think up a pretty good story for this one. Shouldn't be too hard. It seemed like I was already getting by living above the law I'd sworn to uphold and protect. Stealing wages from hookers wasn't the best example of an officer doing the right thing.

A radio crackled on my hip. I picked it up and held it in my palm while I worked out a plan. A voice broke through the static, pinching my nerves.

"Gutierrez. Checking in," was all it said.

I was still a moment. I knew I couldn't wait too long, had to go with something.

"This is Gutierrez, 89063," I said, reading my officer number from the badge. "I have a situation."

"Elaborate."

"I've been, uh, tracking a broad for prostitution. Found her in a hotel room with her trick. They're not dead, but unresponsive. Overdose maybe."

"Location?"

"Hotel on the corner of 47th and Revello." "Roger. Sending backup."

The radio clicked off and the static gave way to silence. My footsteps thumped on the carpet as I lumbered to the bathroom mirror to look at my reflection again. I was taller this time, more masculine. More powerful. It was taking some time to adjust to the weight and sheer brute of this new body.

But I knew could do this. I could be a cop.

I smiled, satisfied with my new shell.

The End.

CASE #12690

STACY
BY MYLES PAINE

Myles Paine was born in Baltimore and is now happy to once again call the Charm City home. He's a former television producer and a lover of dogs, tequila, and fate. You can follow him on Twitter @notmylespaine.

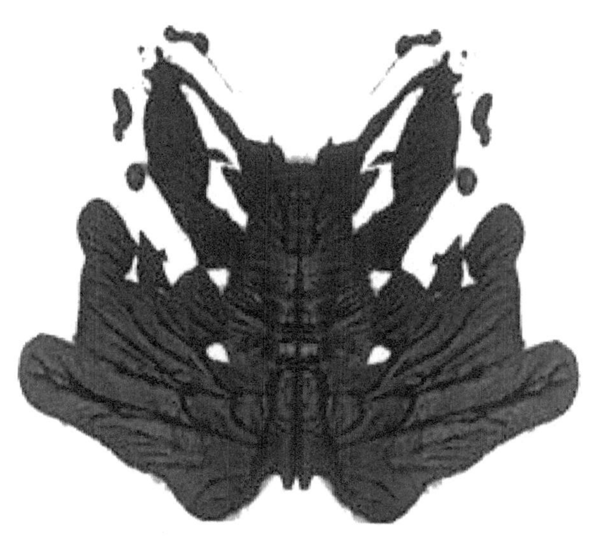

The Third Bell by Ryan Leach

Breathless and frantic, I glanced at my watch; it was 11:57 p.m. The cold, crisp wind tugged at the edges of my coat as the fog descended on the trees that surrounded me. Looking above, I could see the full moon against the pitch black sky. Not a single star was shining, nor did I hear anything besides the sounds of ancient tree branches brushing against each other. Frost had already begun to form on the ground, and the temperature was dropping quickly. I looked at my watch again; the second hand hadn't moved. After closing my eyes and counting to three, I opened them. The hand still didn't move. My disbelief combined with my panic, which was replaced by despair. It felt like a bad dream, except I was awake, and death was coming for me.

My heart hammered inside my chest as I inhaled and exhaled rapidly. I pressed my back against a tree and felt for the knife I wore at my waist. It was there; good. Trembling, I forced myself to breathe slower. I closed my eyes and tried to listen for its footsteps.

What felt like a minute went by and I heard nothing besides my own breathing and heartbeat. The forest was dead silent. I peaked around the edge of the tree; eyes searching the fog for any movement. Holding my breath, I strained myself to find something, anything, but nothing moved. I released my pent up breath and slid to a sitting position against the tree. I wanted to cry, but my terror told me that wasn't a good idea. Whatever was out there was searching for me. If I moved or made a sound, it could mean my discovery. I knew the temperature would get down to the negative degrees and my hunting jacket wouldn't protect me from the elements. I put the hood up and brought my knees to my chest. I had to think of something. Tears began to well up in my eyes. Don't cry, I told myself. Don't make a sound. Maybe I would wake up, just to find out this was a dream.

But then I heard it scream.

My heart stopped as my blood froze in my veins.

I heard a woman screaming out in desperation; bloodcurdling and chilling, almost frantic. It echoed through the trees. It was a scream that intended to cause terror. And it worked.

I opened my eyes and slowly stood up. The thing wailed again, this time sounding closer. I thought I could hear the crunching of frozen grass, slowly getting closer. My body started trembling in fear. I thought to myself, either run and possibly get away, or hide, and hope it doesn't find me. Both choices seemed like suicide, but this creature must know the woods; it would find me eventually. If I ran, I at least had some chance of escape.

I slowly peeked around the edge of the tree in the direction of the last scream and witnessed a dark shape in the fog. Rough patches of long, dark hair sat atop a pale, balding head with what looked like abnormally long arms and legs. It was stepping slowly, turning its head constantly; searching. The creature turned towards the tree I hid behind, the moonlight revealing a twisted pale body. I turned my head back towards the trees in front of me as I hear it scream once more. Without another moment to think, I bolted from my hiding place.

Adrenaline took over as I sprinted through the trees. It cried out, and gave chase. I could hear its feet pounding the earth as I bounded over fallen logs and fought my way through branches that tried to slow me. Twigs snapped behind me as it began to close the distance. It was when I heard it start to laugh that I knew it was about to overtake me. It was a laugh of victory; a hellish sound that still haunts my dreams. My heart was pounding in terror, as if it was trying to escape my chest. I felt my legs burning, and my lungs cried out for air. I couldn't run forever. With a grunt, it slashed out with a clawed hand, ripping the cloth of my jacket. Pain shot through my back, and I knew it had broken skin. I reached for my knife, pulling it from its sheath. Turning quickly, I stabbed towards my pursuer. My blade met nothing but air as I stumbled forwards. The creature was nowhere to be seen, and the woods were silent.

I stopped and looked down at my knife. It was clean. What just happened? Had I imagined the whole thing? No, it was too real. Shaking my head in disbelief, I quickly surveyed my surroundings. There was no life to be seen, but there was a break in the trees up ahead. I had no idea what was on the other side, but I ran for it.

I burled through the trees and stumbled into a frosty wheat field, and saw there was a farm on the other side. I ran towards it, stumbling on the hard clumps of frozen dirt. After making it halfway to the farm house I stopped and turned around. I didn't see any sign of life. The woods were dead silent. Nothing moved except for the leaves which blew in the soft wind. I turned back and ran for the farm.

I reached the farm and heard the sound of dogs barking. The lights inside the house came alive and a man emerged, pointing a shotgun at my chest.

"Stop! That's close enough!" shouted the man as he approached me. I instantly threw my hands in the air and backed up a few steps. The man's dogs, both hounds, were still barking and snarling at me through his window. "What the hell are you doing trespassing on my property?! And in the middle of the night? Are you trying to rob me?!"

"Please don't shoot! I'm just out here hunting with some friends! We were camping in the woods when a thing attacked us!" I shouted as I took a tentative step forward. "Please. My name is-" The words stopped dead on my tongue as I realized that I couldn't remember my name. What is my name? Why can't I remember my name? I lowered my arms and looked quickly at my watch. The second hand was moving. It was 12:13.

"Never mind your name. You said something attacked you?" the man said as he lowered his gun.

"Yeah, and it cut me too!" I turned to show him the back of my coat, and the blood that was soaked into it. "See, I was attacked!"

I saw fear flash in his eyes.

"Was it her?"

"Her? Wait, you know what I'm talking about?"

The man suddenly looked panicked. He grabbed me by the arm and led me to his door, all the while staring out towards the forest, whose ominous trees swayed gently in the wind.

I was greeting by his two drooling dogs as we entered into his home. The entryway was small, with one set of stairs leading to the basement and a hallway leading to the living room. Two pairs of weathered work boots sat next to the door, and I began to take mine off. The front door had three locks, a deadbolt, a chain, and a key lock. The man preceded to lock each one. The locks bothered me; could he be trying to keep that monster out?

He led me into his kitchen and sat me down at the table. He propped his gun against the edge of the table, and I noticed that he didn't unload it. The two hounds sat at my feet, smelling and sniffing the stranger in their home. Looking around, I could see various pictures of a younger version of him with a woman and a baby boy, no older than two. Carved wooden horses and other knickknacks lines the shelves and countertops of his kitchen.

He opened a cupboard and pulled out a first aid kit, and handed me some gauze and tape. He took my coat and took back the first aid supplies, and made a makeshift bandage. My wound still throbbed, but I pushed the pain to the back of my mind. He sat down across from me.

"I'm sorry about the gun, but you just can't be too safe," he said as he leaned forward in his chair. "My name is Josh, and I think I know what you saw out there."

"Really? How could you know?" I said. "You've seen it before?"

"Yes, I've seen her many times over the years. She usually only shows up when the fog rolls in. Sometimes she'll cross the field, and stand on the edge of the property. She never crosses the line though. She just stares, but I swear I've seen her cry, or what I think is her crying. And then she'll scream, and the dogs go crazy. Then I'll go out there with my gun, and she'll disappear back into the fog. She haunts those woods. Then again, nobody would know, I suppose. Nobody ever goes out there. Too creepy, I imagine..." Deep sadness hung in his eyes as he spoke of her. With a jolt, I realized something.

"You know her. What is she?!"

Josh looked me in the eye, and single tear fell from his eye. I looked at the picture of his family again, more specifically at the woman; a tall girl with a long face and long, dark hair.

"She was my wife."

"How? What happened?" I asked. How could this be? Could that woman in the picture really be this terrifying creature?

Josh looked towards the photo, and released a tired sigh. He stood up from the table and walked over to the fridge, opening it, and taking out a bottle of whiskey. He took two glasses from the cupboard over and set them down on the table, filling them halfway. He slid the glass over to me, where I held it, and finally took a swallow. My throat stung from the alcohol. Placing the glass back down, I looked toward Josh. He had already emptied his glass and began to pour another.

"Her name was Amanda. I had known her since we were just kids back in elementary school. It wasn't until freshman year of high school that I finally got the balls to tell her how I felt about her..." Josh said as he took another drink. He gazed out the window, seemingly stuck in a trance.

"Josh," I said.

"Oh yes, sorry. I knew her since we were kids-"

"I know, you just told me. You were saying how you told her how you felt..."

"Yes, yes. I'm sorry. When I told her how I felt, she told me she had had a crush on me since junior high, and that she felt the same. Four years later, just after we graduated, we were married. I started this farm when I was twenty two, and Amanda ran a little business selling crafts and tutoring kids in math. She was so bright, and so talented." Josh took another sip from his glass, and pushed it aside.

"What happened?" I asked.

"After we had our son, she said she started to feel sick. We went to the hospital, but they said it was just some postpartum sickness, and she would feel better in a few weeks. Well, it just got worse from there. A year passed, and she had lost thirty pounds. I feared it was cancer, but it was much worse. She started to sleepwalk, and I would find her in the most random places around our farm. One morning, she was asleep in our bathroom tub, with dirt and leaves matted into her hair. I took her to a psychiatrist to see if there was some mental disorder she had that we could treat. I just wanted her back to normal, but the goddamn shrink said she was just experiencing too much stress and that she would quit the sleepwalking when the stress was eliminated," Josh closed his eyes, and I could see a tear fall.

"But, that doesn't explain how she turned into that thing in the woods," I said as I finished my glass. More tears had begun to fall from Josh's eyes. He looked up, and I noticed his eyes were blue.

"Well, the stress wasn't actually stress. She was being haunted, or cursed. She told me she had started having dreams about a monster stalking her through the woods, and one night she screamed in the middle of us sleeping. She was crying and screaming like a banshee, saying something had killed her in her dream. She said it had whispered to her how it would kill her the next night. She refused to tell me how, and I just assumed it was a nightmare and told her to forget about it, and that it was just a dream. The next night, I stayed awake when we went to bed, and when she started to sleepwalk, I followed her. She went outside, and started to walk towards those fuckin' woods. That was when the fog started to roll in," he said. The tears stopped, and a look of fear replaced the sadness in his eyes.

"There was another one?"

"Yes. And it killed my wife."

"H...how?"

"It lunged out from the fog, and grabbed her. I ran towards it, yelling Amanda's name. The thing ripped open her throat, and marked itself with her blood. It threw her body to the ground, like trash. It turned to me, and I could see its eyes glowing through the fog. I ran, like a coward. I just fucking ran. I left my wife to bleed out in the dirt." The fear in his eyes had glazed over into a stare. I suddenly felt goosebumps rise on my arms. I was scared of him, and I didn't know why.

"It chased me to my house, almost like it was toying with me. It laughed this creepy fucking laugh that made me want to piss myself. I ran into the house and slammed the door, locking it as the dogs ran to me. I heard scratching and clawing on the front door and all I could think about was my son. I ran to his room and I couldn't hear my dogs barking. I threw open the door and there it was, holding my son. Before I could move, it vanished." Tears began to well up in his eyes again.

"It took your son?"

"Yes. And when I finally managed the courage to go back outside for my wife's body, I swear I could hear him crying out there. I called the police, but they didn't believe a single word. Instead, they took me to jail, and later I went to prison for ten years for some bullshit murder charge. They didn't even let me go to her funeral. They just buried her in the cemetery by the old church in town."

"I'm so sorry Josh. That was so cruel of them. But that thing, though. It must still be out there, right?" I said as I leaned forward. "It could still have your son!"

"No, because when I was released, I just came back here. Nobody had done anything with the house. It was like time had stopped here. I bought two new dogs to replace the dead ones. Yeah, nobody had done anything about the dogs." Josh snapped and both of the dogs approached his feet and laid down. He reached for the bottle and brought it to his lips, and drank three swallows before setting it back down. His eyes met mine, and I felt like I was suddenly being watched from every angle. He held my stare as I shifted uncomfortably in my chair.

"Are...are you ok, Josh?" I asked nervously. He didn't blink, nor did his stare waver.

"That night she came, and I didn't know what to do. I thought I was seeing things, but you saw her too. She's here, somewhere. More than likely she'll come back tonight, or tomorrow. Whatever the case, you should stay here until morning." He stood up from the table and took a lurched back a step before regaining his balance. He motioned for me to follow, and he led me into a bedroom. It looked like a child's bedroom, but with a normal sized bed. He stumbled out of the room, almost as if he was in a hurry. I couldn't shake the feeling of begin watched, and the fact that I was sleeping in a stranger's room after being attacked was still surreal to me. I sat down on the bed, and looked out the window towards the woods. I searched for fog and movement, but saw neither. I stretched out on the bed, and somehow fell asleep.

In my dream, I was being chased by a dark fog through a never-ending forest. I felt the coldness of the fog begin to envelop me, and as I opened my mouth to yell, I heard that bone chilling scream.

My eyes jerked open, and I couldn't believe my eyes.

It was standing over me.

I opened my mouth to scream, but it lashed out a claw towards my neck, ripping it open. I clutched at my throat and felt the hot blood flow between my fingers. I tried frantically to lash out, but it leaned closer, dark hair just inches from my face. I was paralyzed. Its distorted face was barely reminiscent of the girl I saw in the photo. Blind eyes looked into mine, and graying lips pulled apart to reveal a blackened smile. Dark blood began to drip from its eyes onto my skin, and where the droplets landed, the skin turned a sickly pale gray. It turned towards my ear.

"The third bell will ring, and you will die," it whispered in a deep female voice. It dipped a cold, black claw into the blood that escaped between my fingers and traced an obscure glyph upon its own neck. It then proceeded to draw strange patterns from the glyph to a marking on its chest. My vision began to darken and the creature screamed again with glee, its eyes bleeding profusely. It slowly became transparent and then it was gone. I went limp, and everything faded to black.

I jerked awake and grasped at my neck. I felt the smooth skin and the shape of my Adam's apple, but no blood or open wound. There was nothing. I sat up and ran to the living room where I saw Josh sitting on the couch in front of the TV, watching the news and holding a beer. He looked haggard, but awake.

"Josh-,"

"I told you she would come, didn't I?" he said as he turned towards me, glazed over eyes looking into mine. He stood up and walked right past me. I followed him into the kitchen, where he finally stopped. He stood next to the table, and I noticed that he hadn't put the gun away from the previous night.

"Josh, I don't know if she was, but I had the most terrifying dream about her, it felt so real…" I said. Josh turned towards me, wearing a deranged smile. His glazed over eyes were now replaced with a psychotic, almost insane look. He started to shake, back convulsing, and I realized he was repressing laughter. I took a step back, suddenly feeling very afraid, and sensing something was about to happen. His giggles turned to laughter, and he fell to his knees, unable to contain his insanity any longer.

"I think I should leave-,"

"YOU KNOW WE ARE BOTH DEAD, RIGHT?!" Josh screamed as he scrambled up from the floor. His eyes were wide, and his hand shot towards the gun. I backtracked a few steps and threw my hands into the air. He aimed the shotgun at my chest, and clicked the safety off.

"Josh, please!"

"She already killed you!! And now she wants ME! Don't you get it?! We are both DEAD. DEAD!!" Josh screamed as he pumped a shell into the chamber. He took a step towards me, gun barrel now pointing towards my head.

"Nobody is dead, Josh! Just let me go and we can call the police! Just put down the gun, please!" I cried as he pushed the barrel to my forehead. I sank to my knees, tears streaming down my face.

"She already has you, and I won't let her take me!!" he said as he lowered the barrel from my head. With a sick realization, I knew what he was about to do. He stuck the end of the shotgun in his mouth, and rolled his eyeballs back, so just the whites were visible.

"Josh!"

His finger moved, and before I could react, blood splattered and painted the ceiling above us. His body fell backwards, and the gun with it. The hounds barked and ran from their fallen owner.

I stared at his body for minutes, unable to comprehend what I just witnessed. This man had taken me into his home in the middle of the night, and now he laid dead in front of me. His blood was beginning to pool when I finally raised myself from my knees. Josh's hounds walked over to their master, sniffing his body as I slowly approached. Part of me expected him to jump up, brandishing his shotgun and pumping a round into my chest, but the rational part of me knew he was dead and wouldn't be getting up.

I timidly approached the door, glancing back at Josh's fallen figure. I took the keys to his truck off a key rack by the door as I whispered a silent prayer for him. I left the house, got into his truck, and drove to the nearest town.

As I got to the town, its name I do not know, I broke out in tears. I wondered what had I done in my life to deserve this terror that had seized me. I had committed the same sins as everyone else, but why was I being hunted? I had just gone on a simple hunting trip with some friends. They had told me this forest held the best deer in Minnesota.

But that's when she came.

The thing had come upon us at roughly 11 p.m. We had gone back to the trucks and our campsite. We had a few beers, played some cards, and talked about our hunt. That's when it struck. It came out of the woods like a ghost and before I knew what was happening two of my friends were dead. The other two and I ran. We somehow got split up and I don't know what happened to them, and I hope one day I will, if this curse ever leaves me.

I dried my tears and got out of the car. I walked towards the nearest building in the town; a gas station. I entered and asked the oily teenager behind the counter where the police department was. He said most of the cops would be at the church, discussing the recent thefts there. He pointed me in the right direction and I headed there immediately.

The church was ancient and enormous. Its sheer size left me in awe. It was made of dark colored wood with large ominous windows. A golden cross sat upon a large bell, which was at the very top. The bell itself was large and shined dully in the sunlight. I approached the large doors and knocked twice. Within a few seconds a police officer opened the door and gave me a strange look.

"How can I help you, sir?" he asked as he examined me. The other two cops in the church stopped their conversation with what I assumed was the pastor of the church. They looked towards me and pointed.

"I, uh, need to report an attack and a suicide," I said as the other two cops joined the one I was speaking to.

"Attack? On whom?" one of the officers asked.

"A group of hunters I was part of. A monster attacked us at night. Something supernatural," I attempted to explain. They looked at each other and smirked.

"Sir, were you by chance intoxicated, or perhaps, using illegal narcotics when this 'thing' attacked you and your group?" one of the cops asked me.

"Or perhaps tell us about the other incident; the suicide," said the first cop.

"His wife was being haunted or cursed by some monster, and it killed her. Somehow, she came back, but now she is that monster. She's been haunting him for years, and while my friends and I were camping, she attacked us and chased me through the woods. I ran to this farm, and the owner let me in, but he was acting all weird. She somehow got inside, and killed me, but in a dream. He knew she was there, and he snapped. He threatened me with a shotgun and starting saying how we were both dead. Before I could do anything, he shot himself!" I sputtered out. I realized how idiotic I sounded when all the cops laughed at my statement. The pastor looked concerned, and walked through the cops and pulled me aside.

"Allow me to have a word with him, officers," said the pastor.

They snorted and he pulled me into the plaza in front of the church.

"What exactly-," said the pastor as the bell at the top of the church began to ring.

My stomach dropped and my knees buckled. My throat started to burn. A sharp pain erupted in my chest. The pastor screamed something, but I couldn't hear him.

The second bell rang and I dropped to my hands and knees, coughing up blood and shaking violently. The burning on my throat began to take a pattern. My thoughts flickered back to the pattern the creature had formed on its throat.

The third bell rang.

The pattern burned and itched intensely. My body began to convulse and my eyes welled up with blood. Droplets slowly leaked from my eyes. I couldn't feel my heart beating anymore. Looking up, I saw a woman walking towards me, and I recognized her as the creature, but she wasn't in a hideous form. Time seemed to stand still as she approached me. She had long black hair and light skin, dressed in a flowing black dress. In her hands she held a black bird. Her beauty was marred only by the drops of blood that also flowed from her eyes, and the pattern on her neck that glowed a deep crimson.

She lightly touched my cheek with one elegant hand, and slid it down to the pattern on my neck. It burned as her fingers danced across it. She bent down and looked into my eyes, and she smiled.

"The curse is now yours," she whispered as she rested her hand upon mine. My convulsions began to cease. I looked down at my hands to see that they were becoming transparent. A faint black glow was starting to surround them.

"With the ringing of the third bell, your death has freed me, and now I am able to move on to the next life," she said to me, her eyes full of sorrow. She leaned towards me and kissed my cheek, and stood up. I too, stood up, and saw my body lying on the ground. Blood trickled out of my mouth as the pastor knelt by my side and the police calling for help. I looked at my graying hands and saw they had become elongated. She handed me the black bird, which gazed up at me. Its eyes glowed red.

Amanda smiled at me one last time, and then faded into nothing. Her voice echoed in my head as I looked from the bird to my reflection in the pooling blood. I fell to my knees, raised the bird in my hands, and screamed.

The End.

CASE #31730

THE THIRD BELL
BY RYAN LEACH

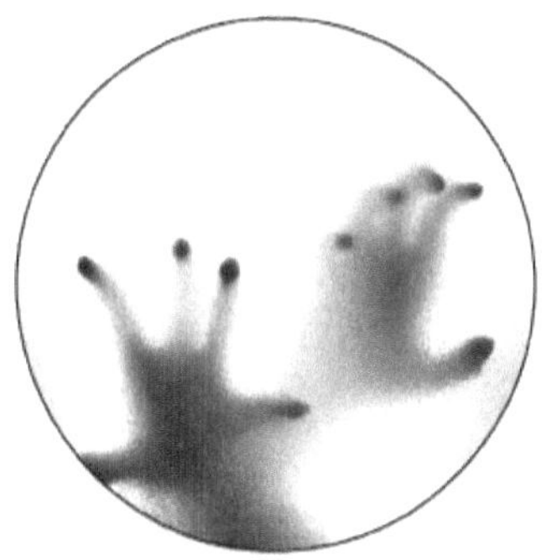

Details not released at this time

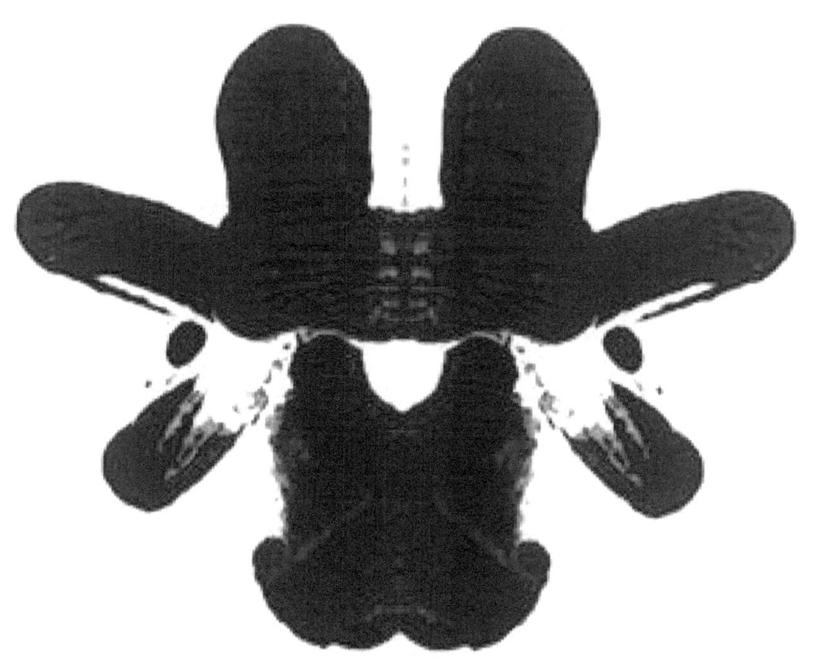

Leper Writer by Roo Bardookie

The stench of the rotting meat of me filled my senses. It was
so bad I rarely smelled the others.

Thank God for Father Damien here on our prison of an island.

Today I am going to write about. . .

a dog comes into the cave, and smells the meat from the dying
man, walks up and sniffs, and takes his last fingers, which he
had trained to hold the quill

The dog ate the fingers, all of the fingers, until just the pads of
the man's hands were left

and that is how we was able to narrate the rest of the piece,
while as he is writing this, the dog continues to chew his digits

he vomits out the bones and continues on until the next meat
man appears to him, where he will gorge until it comes up

CASE #50195

LEPER WRITER

BY ROO BARDOOKIE

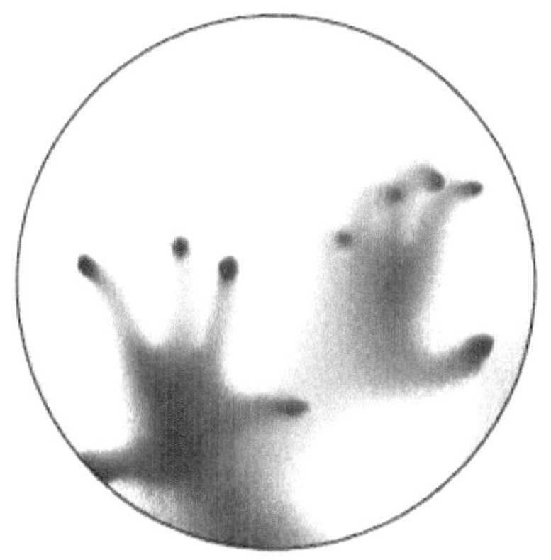

Details not released at this time

On the
Record

A Moment With Jeff Menapace

Jeff: tell us about your upbringing in Philly! Being a city with a pretty dark past that many don't know about (slave markets, notorious prisons), did it or does it bring you inspiration for your work?

Not really. I grew up primarily in the suburbs and am shamefully ignorant when it comes to the city of Philadelphia's history…with the exception of Joe Frazer (Big boxing fan).

When did you know you wanted to write horror fiction and non-fiction?

Non-fiction came about with my interest in martial arts. I was able to get a few articles published in martial arts magazines before I even attempted publishing my fiction. Now, as for thriller and horror fiction, I've been writing that as long as I can remember. When I was a kid, it wasn't unusual for teachers to call home and tell my mother about a "somewhat disturbing" story I wrote for class. Good times.

Do you have a particularly ritual or routine when it comes to sitting down and writing? How long, would you say, does it take you to lay out the story before the actual writing begins? Or do you just let the words flow from the start?

More the latter than the former, however I always have at least some idea of where the story is going. Generally, my stories start with an idea and I build on them from there, day to day. I'm not much of an outliner as I am a Post-it notes freak — my office looks like Staples ransacked it. I can definitely say that

more often than not, my stories end up going in a different direction than what I'd initially thought. But that's the fun of the whole process if you ask me. Copying directly from an intensive outline feels too much like work. Coming to the keyboard each day not knowing what to expect is one of the great thrills of writing for me. A great example would be Stephen King's admission on how Misery played out. He'd initially thought it would be a novella with an ending that saw Paul Sheldon dying at the hands of Annie Wilkes. But as he began writing, he found the Sheldon character to be far more resourceful and decided to go in a completely different direction. The same thing often happens to me. A character that I'd initially planned to be minor, and possibly killed, begins to grow on me, and next thing I know he's playing a major part in the story.

Your short stories you say are written when your brain is in the "off switch." Why does writing short stories help revitalize your longer pieces and what makes them unique?

Good question. I guess that answer would be that I'm always thinking of new story ideas, and sometimes those stories are better told short than long. I'd also say that even if I wasn't writing for a living, I'd still be doing it for fun. So, when my brain refuses to let a story idea go, I sit down and write it because it's what I love to do. If I feel—like the Stephen King/Misery example I mentioned above—like the story is going to be more complex as it unfolds, then it ends up becoming a novel. I always stick to the belief that the story is done when it's done, long or short.

You're active on social media, which must be great for your fans. Do you like being able to interact with your audience so easily?

Absolutely! I would be nothing without my fans. I would

wager that every writer gets down in the dumps about their talent from time to time, yet when you get emails or messages etc. telling you how much they love your work, it makes it all worthwhile. As a result, I try to give back and communicate with my readers as much and as often as possible. For example, I have a newsletter (sign up at jeffmenapace.com pretty please) where I am always giving away free goodies or giving sneak peeks on future works as a show of thanks.

On that same note, how has the explosion of self-publishing and eBooks affected your career as a writer?

It is my career! When I decided I wanted to try and write for a living, I started down the traditional route. I published short fiction here and there and collected my share of rejection slips on my novels. I did get some pretty big bites on a couple of my books, but ultimately the publishers ended up passing. Not long after, I was very fortunate to land an agent. Again, we went the traditional route of pitching to publishers with many nibbles but alas, no bites. Around this time I began self-publishing some of the short fiction I'd been writing during the interim and was surprised to see it doing rather well. After nearly two years with my agent, I finally decided to take the big leap, part ways, and go out on my own with indie publishing. It was a very terrifying prospect, but I'd done a great deal of homework. Fortunately, my debut novel Bad Games did well and I was able to build from there.

Congratulations on all the interest in Bad Games as feature films. Do you have an update for us that you can share?

Oh how I wish I did. The only thing I can say at this time is that I did sign an optioning agreement with a producer for all three books in the trilogy. I cross my fingers and toes daily, and not an 11:11 goes by without my wishing to see my books up on the big screen. How amazing that would be.

Similarly, how do you feel about letting someone else take the reign on your ideas and turn it into a visual telling of your work?

I think it's both exciting and nerve-wracking. Exciting to see someone's interpretation of your work on the big screen, and nerve-wrecking for fear that it'll turn out to be a steaming pile of poo and nothing like the book I wrote. But it is my understanding that that's the way it goes in Hollywood: very few writers get to weigh in creatively on the film project to be sure Hollywood is giving their work the proper respect they think it deserves. Being a bit of a control freak, I imagine it's something I'm going to have to get used to. But hey, I call those champagne problems; I'll just be happy if the books get made into film.

You're a horror writer, yet you hate spiders! Do you have any other fears or phobias? Have you ever used them in your writing?

I'm actually getting better with spiders! My wife and I now live in a more rural area of Pennsylvania, and spiders are definitely more aplenty. I'm not ready to hold one yet, but I'm getting better! As for other phobias, I can't say I have any now, but I did as a kid. I had a fear of deformities, and the film The Elephant Man scared the hell out of me. I made the main male protagonist, Patrick, suffer from the same childhood phobia in Bad Games. I think I was sixteen before I could watch The Elephant Man again and was delightfully shocked at what a great film it was. Oh, and for the record, I saw the film Arachnophobia and loved it, so I guess that's progress too.

What would you tell an emerging author about what it's like to break into the industry? Any advice to heed or advice to disregard?

My advice probably won't be anything they haven't heard already, and that is to keep reading and writing, and never, ever give up. Do your homework—marketing is ridiculously vital in indie publishing—and don't fear rejection. Believe in yourself and keep plugging away. If you're good, you'll get there

eventually. Nothing is impossible if you put the time and effort in. When I was trying to get published, I was teaching grammar school. I used to get up two hours early (not easy when you are anything but a morning person) and write before heading off to teach. I was that determined to make it. I would also urge people to look at someone like Hugh Howey. He self-published a

short story (Wool) in 2011, and look at him now. While he might be considered the exception rather than the rule, he is certainly a great example of talent and hard work taking you places you might have previously thought impossible.

A Moment With Dan Sunley: Pieces

Thanks for speaking with us, Dan! Tell us a little bit about yourself: where are you from, and with Pieces being your directorial debut, how did you decide to make the jump?

Thanks for having me, this is my first ever interview - so I'm honoured! I'm from a small town in East Yorkshire, had a college education in Theatre but always wanted to do something related movies. In 2006 I wrote and produced a low-budget feature with no idea and made all the mistakes, but it was great experience. For the last three years I've taken a break from a 'real' job to get a boost on studying/writing screenplays. The nature screenwriting (especially spec's) can feel a little stoic; I wanted a change of pace and some practical experience so I tried to create an interesting short script that could be done on a small budget. I thought making a short film would be easier than the crushing-nerve-panic of pitching stories to executives, it wasn't *that* easy, but I was half right - at least at the moment.

**You're very much into the supernatural and horror –
why the interest? Where did that come from for you?**

Seeing Ghostbusters as a young child was probably the main
culprit for the fascination of the supernatural. I didn't discover the
rush of horror movies until my early twenties; I loved how the
psychological journeys stayed with me long after the initial
viewing, when I turned the lights off. My mother has actually
had a genuine paranormal experience with an ouija board once,
so I don't think there has been any doubt in our family that
there are things out there beyond our current understanding.

**What is the one, quintessential Asian horror film every movie
buff should see?**

It's a coin toss between Kim Jee-woon's "Tale of Two Sisters"
and Ahn Beyong Ki's "Phone" I reckon most buffs will have
seen the former so the latter is worth checking out. If only for
one of the creepiest performances you'll ever see out of
someone under the age of 10, it also has a good twist, they truly
are the masters at the Supernatural Thriller genre.

**You also say your inspiration comes from movie and video
game soundtracks. How important is it to you when picking
music for movies and how does that process work for you?**

I don't what I'd listen to if I didn't have soundtracks. My
screenplay ideas usually start with a single scene that comes
from listening to instrumentals (I have headphones on
everywhere I walk). I create playlists that score the movie
while I'm writing. A lot of my music is organised by the

images they create i.e. I have playlists for dark nights, icy landscapes, daytimes, tension, that sort of thing. For me it's about creating an environment where you can put yourself inside the idea and then see where your imagination takes you.

On that same note, what is your favorite video game? And your favorite video game soundtrack?

Don't make me choose!! Okay, the original Sonic The Hedgehog (you never forget your first love), my favourite game soundtrack would be Metal Gear Solid or Final Fantasy XIII-2. I have some weird stuff.

Are you still writing? What are the challenges of directing compared to your work putting pen to paper?

I think I will always write. Although time at the desk has taken a back seat as the Pieces project has gone on. Screenwriting is like playing chess with yourself; you have all the time in the world to work on your methods, read how to's, build strategies, get feedback and re-evaulate your work. Directing feels like playing three chess games against three real opponents, you're also against the clock and all the pieces can move randomly

after each turn! Not having a plan will instantly lead to ruin but you can't turn up to set with blinkers on. You have to be flexible, not all of your ideas/shots will work; but story/action trumps all other aspects; if you don't have the coverage that connects your story points together you'll get into tricky waters during the edit. Your audience will forgive a few continuity errors (like a tea cup that moves between shots) they won't forgive a story that doesn't make any sense.

The premise of Pieces is intriguing, eerie and seems to be able to encompass an ending to suit every viewer. Will there be big twists in this movie or are you a fan of letting the fans piece together the conclusion (if you'll mind the pun!)?

I hope so! I think by design short films leave the audience to draw their own conclusions more than features. You don't have the time to explain every what/why/how - and there's a nice bit of creative freedom in that, they are fantastic for creating debate afterwards. I hope to give the viewer a flavour of emotional content and just enough information that they can form their own mental investigation during the film, I guess the proof of the pudding will be if they get emotionally involved and not think: "what was the point in that?" I sincerely hope it's the former.

When will Pieces premier, and how can people see it?

We don't have premier date yet as such. We're editing over Christmas and finishing post in the New Year, we'll then submit to 2016's film festivals which will (hopefully) show the film around next Autumn.

What can we expect from you in the next year? Five years? Ten years? Do you have on penultimate career milestone that you'd like to achieve?

Hopefully more movies! I'd like to direct another short, build on working relationships, experience and continue to learn. My main goal is to try and build the steps to enable be able to write/direct a feature in the future. My ultimate career goal would be to have a film under the Blumhouse banner - I love the way they produce their movies.

You're a self-proclaimed Daniel Craig Bond fan. Have you seen Spectre? What did you think?

It was good, wasn't it! I think it was the James Bond movie the James Bond fans wanted to see; it seemed closer to the format of the older ones, which is no bad thing but to me it felt like the odd one out of all Craig's Bonds, I don't know why though. Casino Royale is still my favourite.

Are there any directors / writers that you think we should be looking out for?

Ti West is one. Adam Winguard is another, I read that he's taking on the live-action re-make of Death Note, so that'll be interesting. It'll be great to see what Robert David Mitchell comes up with next if he stays in the horror genre. James Wan goes with out saying doesn't he?

If you could direct / reboot any screenplay what would it be?

I always thought Let's Scare Jessica to Death (1971) would be an interesting film to update, it's 44 years old but it has a different spin on an old trope.

Finally, do you have any must have items or rituals for a shoot (superstitious or otherwise) before it goes ahead?

I just try to get some quiet time, somewhere unfamiliar. For me it's sitting in a coffee shop or taking a walk somewhere, alone. Give yourself a little time to take a breath before the chaos starts.

Photography by Alan G. Mather

Hello horror lover.
If you've been suffering from a persistent desire for just a little more unpleasantness in your life, we have the answer:
NOCTURNAL TRANSMISSIONS
NOCTURNAL TRANSMISSIONS
PODCAST
Nocturnal Transmissions is a fortnightly podcast featuring inspired performances of dark tales both old and new by voice artist Kristin Holland.
Find them at
nocturnaltransmissions.com.au
or wherever good podcasts are purveyed.

If you have any feedback or would like to leave a review please head over to Amazon and share your thoughts about Sanitarium.

Thank you for your time and we salute your love for all things horror.

https://www.facebook.com/SanitariumPublishing

https://www.thesanitarium.co.uk/

https://twitter.com/sanitariumlit

https://www.instagram.com/sanitariumpublishing/